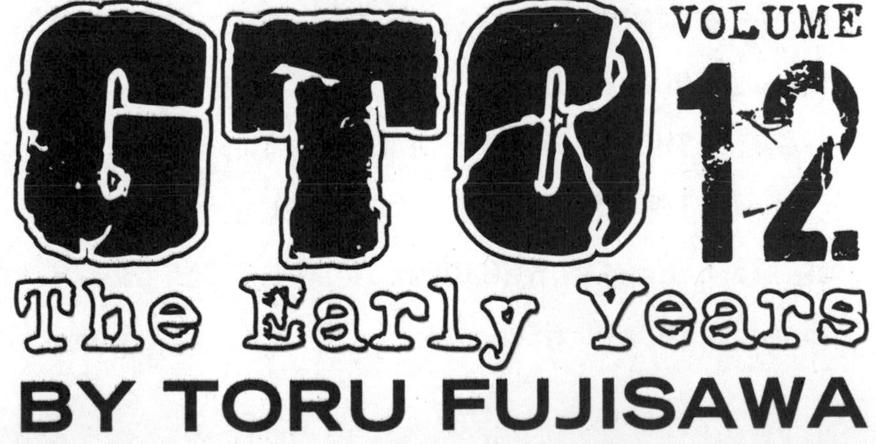

# GTO The Early Years
VOLUME 12

BY TORU FUJISAWA

# CONTENTS

GTO The Early Years
Chapter 198: YESTERDAY'S WOMAN, TODAY'S WOMAN
B. B.Q

AHA-HA-HA!
KYA-HA-HA!

THANK YOU VERY MUCH!
RATTLE

ALL RIGHT, ONE MORE BAR?
OH, WE CAN'T, RYUJI! YOU'RE STILL IN HIGH SCHOOL!

IT'S FINE! ANYWAY, IT'S NOT LIKE I'M YOUR STUDENT ANY-MORE.

YOU'RE ALL GUNG-HO JUST BECAUSE I'M TREAT-ING!
Don't elders usually treat?!
What?!

BUT IT'S KIND OF STRANGE...

WHAT IS?

IT'S BEEN FOREVER SINCE WE LAST MET
BUT I CAN TALK TO YOU SO NATU-RALLY.

TO BE HONEST...
I HAD CONSIDERED SLUGGING YOU IF WE EVER MET AGAIN.

BUT THE MOMENT I SAW YOU, THAT ALL SUDDENLY SEEMED SO STUPID.
MAYBE TIME REALLY DOES HEAL ALL WOUNDS, HUH?
...
LOOKING BACK, ALL I CAN REMEMBER ARE THE GOOD TIMES WE HAD TOGETHER.
...
I HAD THOUGHT THAT I SHOULDN'T TRY TO RE-MEMBER...
THAT I HAD TO FORGET ... FOR GOOD ...
BUT, WELL ...
THAT DIDN'T SEEM TO WORK.
HALT
GRIP
INFORMATION
REST ¥4.500-
LODGING ¥6.800-
サービスタイム AM8:00~PM4:00 ¥4,500(2時間)
HOTEL NEWYORK
HOW ABOUT ...
WE DROP BY HERE?

WHAT ?
I HAD THOUGHT THAT LEAVING THE WAY I DID
WAS BEST FOR YOU, RYUJI.
HOTEL NEW YORK
AFTER THAT, I RETURNED TO MY PARENTS' ...
I THOUGHT I WOULD TEACH AGAIN, AND EVENTUALLY GET MARRIED.
BUT IN THE END, I'VE RETURNED ...
...
TO SHO-NAN.
I JUST CAN'T FORGET ABOUT
YOU, RYUJI.
BUT ...
THERE'S ANOTHER WOMAN I LOVE RIGHT NOW.
THAT'S FINE.
I DON'T MIND BEING YOUR NUMBER TWO, OR ANYTHING ...
JUST AS LONG AS I CAN BE WITH YOU.

A-AYUMI...
I DON'T CARE ABOUT HOW OLD YOU AND I ARE ANYMORE.
I CAN WAIT YEARS EVEN.
I JUST WON'T LET YOU GO AGAIN.
I'VE FINALLY FIGURED THINGS OUT...
WHAT? W-WAIT, AYUMI...
NOW I KNOW MY TRUE FEEL-INGS...
?!

JOLT
シュー
PSHHHH
HAH
コポ
GLOG
コポ
HAH
HAH
HAH

JUST A DREAM?
ふぅー
PHEW
Ahh... don't scare me like that!

SOME-THING WRONG?
HM?
パサッ
PLUNK

DID YOU HAVE A WEIRD DREAM OR SOME-THING?

Y-YEAH. IT'S NOTH-ING, REALLY.
HA HA HA!
Yeah, nothing!
Ha ha ha...

DAMMIT, THOUGH, WHAT A DREAM TO HAVE.
HOW MUCH MORE HOT AND HEAVY COULD IT GET?

OF ALL THINGS, DREAMING TO KISS AYUMI...
WHY SUCH A DREAM?

RYUJ ...
AYU-MI ...
HOOONK
PSHHH
THAT NIGHT ...
HOOONK
...
GRMMM
THAT NIGHT, THAT WAS ALL THAT HAPPENED.
SHE DISAPPEARED BEFORE WE COULD EVEN SAY A WORD. SO WHY ...
She's really in Haya-ma...
HEY, YOU!

SQUEEEEZE
GIRKKK
I TOLD YOU TO SPIT IT OUT! WHAT KIND OF DREAM DID YOU HAVE?!

IT WAS ENOUGH TO MAKE YOU TALK IN YOUR SLEEP, SO IT MUST HAVE BEEN A REALLY STRANGE ONE! RIGHT?
COME ON, OUT WITH IT.

WHAT?! TALKING IN MY SLEEP?

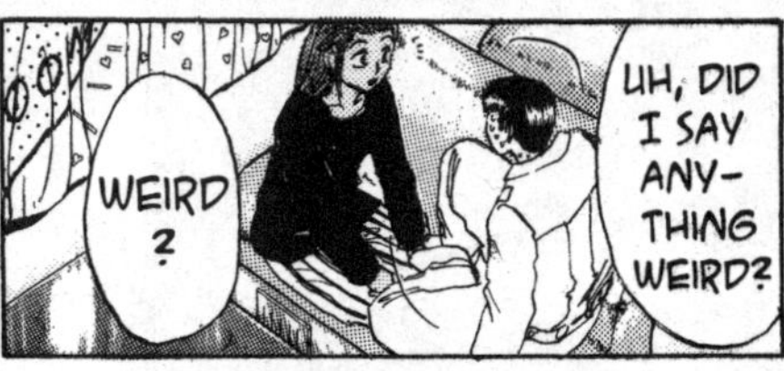
UH, DID I SAY ANY-THING WEIRD?
WEIRD?

L-LIKE MAYBE **some-one's name** OR SOME-THING...

?
WHY?
O-OH, NO REA-SON!
Ha ha ha ha ha
JUST AS LONG AS I DIDN'T!
HOP

HEY, I'M OUT OF SMOKES!

G-GUESS I'LL GO OUT FOR A BIT AND BUY SOME!

MAN, WHAT AM I SAYING?

Hahahaha

HEY! WHO'S NAME?! WAIT...

...

THE "BAKU" IN "ONI-BAKU" IS LEAVING NOW.
ALL THAT'S LEFT IS THAT WOMAN.
FWOMM

WHAT'LL WE DO? THIS IS OUR CHANCE.
WANT US TO GET HER?

I'M TIRED OF SITTING HERE ON LOOK-OUT.
LET'S HAVE SOME FUN, TOO.
Right, Joey?

TWITCH

J-JUST KIDDING. DON'T GLARE AT ME...
Not one for jokes? Heh!
GULP
...

FINE WITH ME. DO IT.

HUH?

MESS DANMA'S WOMAN UP SO BAD THAT SHE'S PRACTI-CALLY IN PIECES.
?!

Flashback sound effect

PWOOM
RYUJI ...
PWOOM
AYUMI ...
Do whatever you want with me...
I will...
...

DAGH! WH-WHAT AM I THINKING?!
BAM
STOMP
BAM
GSSH
DO I REALLY WANT TO GO DOWN THAT DIRTY PATH?!

A-ANYWAY, I'M NOT GOING TO HAYAMA AGAIN.
IT'S SET!

I'VE ALREADY GOT
A GIRL WHO NEEDS ME.
YEAH, RIGHT!
Talking up my girl... How lame!
FWOM
FWOM
SKREE
YO, RYUJI!
SCHT
DWOOM
DWOOM
DWOOM
I WAS JUST ON THE WAY OVER TO YOUR PLACE.
MY PLACE?
I HAVE A GUEST WHO JUST
HAS TO SEE YOU.
HEY.
A GUEST?
SST

SHFF
?!
A-AYUMI!
Grin
STEP
WELL, HERE YOU GO.
SORRY, BUT I'M OUTTA HERE.
BUT IF YOU DO SOMETHING TO MAKE MAYUMI CRY, I'M NOT JUST GONNA KEEP QUIET, OKAY?
HUH? H-HEY, FUMIYA!
BRMMMM
Laters !!
W-WAIT ...
...
...

HAVE YOU BEEN
DO-ING WELL?

...
...

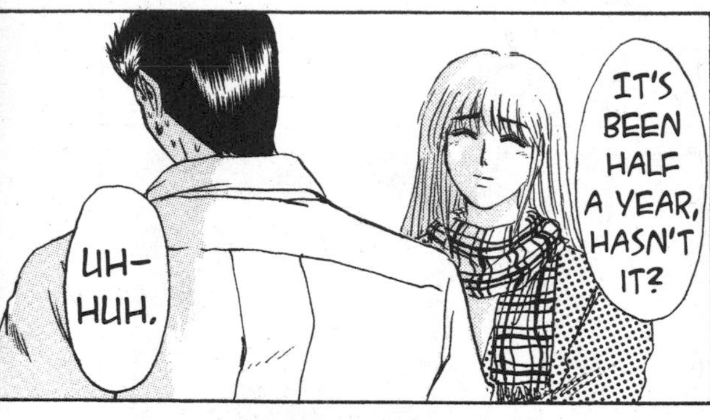
IT'S BEEN HALF A YEAR, HASN'T IT?
UH-HUH.

Y-YEAH...

UH... I-I'M LIKING THE NO-GLASSES LOOK, TOO.
Hahaha...

HUSH
...
...

YOU'VE ALREADY GOT A WOMAN! A DEAR ONE NAMED NAGISA!!

WH-WHAT AM I SAYING?!

SORRY ABOUT THE OTHER DAY.

THANK YOU.

WE HADN'T SEEN EACH OTHER IN HALF A YEAR...
AND WE DIDN'T EVEN GET TO TALK.
I THOUGHT WE OUGHT TO PROPERLY MEET AGAIN.

O-OK...

IT'S COLD HERE, ISN'T IT?
Y-YEAH...

WHY DON'T WE GO SOME-WHERE ELSE?
LIKE WHERE?

How does
my room sound?

HUH?

W-WAIT, IS THAT DREAM ...
SERI-OUSLY COMING TRUE ??
A-AYUMI ...

...

SMIRK

SOMETHING WAS UP WITH RYUJI TODAY.
FLAP
I WONDER IF SOME-THING HAPPEN-ED?

WHAT KIND OF DREAM COULD HE HAVE HAD?

COULD IT HAVE BEEN ...

OH, STOP IT! WHAT AM I THINKING ABOUT?
Yikes, self-loathing!
AAH, COME HOME SOON, RYUJI!
WHUM

KNOCK KNOCK
OH
Ryuji?

RATTLE
YOU TOOK SO LONG!
HOW FAR DID YOU GO TO BUY CIGA—
!

...

HELLO

?!

GRASP

EEEK! WHAT ARE YOU DOING? LET GO OF ME!!
WH-WHO ARE YOU PEOPLE? WHAT DO YOU WANT?

Just pals
of Dan-ma's.

PALS ?!
CUT THE CRAP!

OH, WE'RE PALS ...
BEST PALS

After all, he's going to lead me
to the Stair-way to Heav-en.

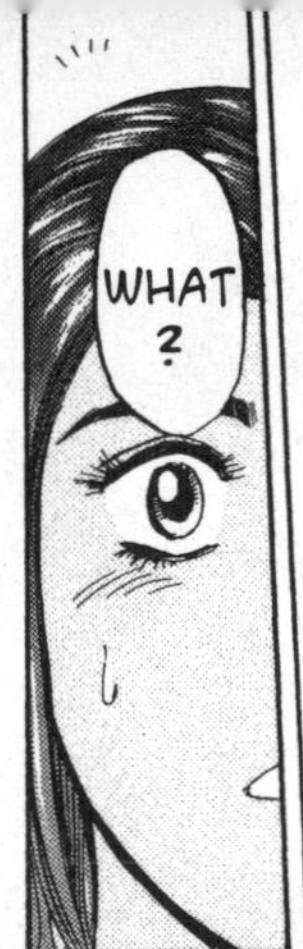
WHAT?

WAIT A SEC ...
WHAT DO YOU MEAN BY THAT?
...?

PRRRR RIIIIIING

YO SAKA-SHITA?
WHAT'S UP?

I'M TAILING DANMA RIGHT NOW, AND...

WHAT?

I THOUGHT WE JUST MIGHT BE ABLE TO USE THIS.

ALL RIGHT, GOT IT. KEEP TAILING HIM.
DON'T LET THEM OUT OF YOUR SIGHT. GOT IT?

After all, *she* is valuable bait, too.

...
SNAP
DASH

SOME-ONE, PLEASE HELP!
H-HEY, WOMAN!

SHHT

BAM
WHAK

HEY!
EEK!
I'LL WRECK IT ALL.

You and every-thing that he holds dear!!
GRIN
...!
I'LL BE OKAY! I KNOW RYUJI WILL COME RESCUE ME!
THAT'S RIGHT! HASN'T RYUJI ALWAYS

SWEPT IN AND RESCUED ME?!

KLAK KLAK
KLAK

KREEK

COME IN.
...
THUMP
THUMP
THUMP

## Chapter 199: ROOM

OH ...
S-SORRY! I'LL MAKE SOME COFFEE, OKAY?
S-SURE ...
WOW, SO YOU'RE LIVING IN HAYAMA, HUH?
FANCY!
NOT AT ALL. I MIGHT BE IN HAYAMA, BUT THIS PLACE IS—
Hm?
I-IT'S NOT BAD AT ALL, IF YOU ASK PLEBS LIKE ME ...
I BET THE VIEW IS GREAT, TOO ...
ガラ
RATTLE
OH, DON'T OPEN THAT!
あーーん
OOOOOH!
AAAAH
いいーっ
YESSS
いやー
NOOO
IT'S ...
RIGHT NEXT TO A LOVE HOTEL.
I said not to...

CLINK
Ecureuil

KLINK
カチャ カチャ
...
KLINK
カチャ カチャ
...

SORRY
DID I ONLY TROUBLE YOU BY ASKING YOU TO COME HERE?

N-NO, THAT'S NOT TRUE AT ALL.
...

WHEN... DID YOU COME BACK?

ABOUT TWO WEEKS AGO.
I'M JUST LIVING IN THIS PLACE TEMPORARILY UNTIL MY NEW LIFE'S SORTED OUT.
HUH

MY PARENTS PESTER ME WHEN I'M AT HOME.
THEY KEEP SAYING, "GET MARRIED!"

I WAS SET UP WITH SOMEONE ... FOR AN ARRANGED MARRIAGE.
...

BUT I TURNED HIM DOWN!!
He he he
SO IT BECAME HARD FOR ME TO LIVE AT HOME.

AND I FINALLY DECIDED TO LEAVE!

NOW, I'M JUST
A REGULAR KINDERGARTEN TEACHER.

R-
REALLY ...

WHAT ABOUT YOU, RYUJI?
HUH?
Have you found a girlfriend,
Ryuji?
HM? N-NO ...
NOT ME ...
NOT YET ...

KLAAANK

WHLIP
FRET
FRET
HOTTT!
HOT HOT HOT!
DRIP
DRIP
DRIB-BLE

OH, YOU'RE AS CLUMSY AS EVER!
WAIT THERE, I'LL BRING A CLOTH.
RISE

WH-WHAT AM I SAYING?
WHY AM I NOT TELLING HER THAT I'M LIVING WITH A WOMAN?!
DRIBBLE

I CAN'T BE THINKING OF TRYING TO GET BACK TOGETHER WITH AYUMI?
THAT'S...

HM?

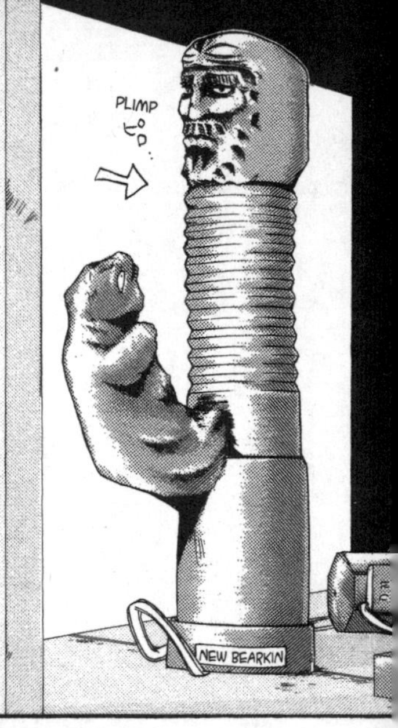
PLIMP
NEW BEARKIN

WHA ?!

WH- WHAT IS THAT BLANTANT-LOOKING PIECE OF FOLK ART?
TREMBLE
COULD THAT BE... "MOMMY'S LITTLE HELPER" ??

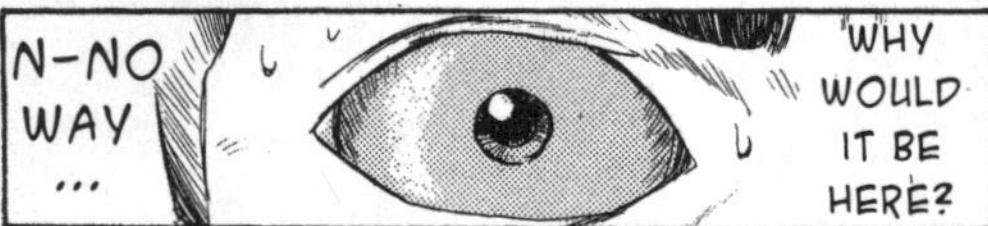
WHY WOULD IT BE HERE?
N-NO WAY ...

AYUMI COULDN'T BE USING THAT, COULD SHE?!
My pure image of her!
ARGH

RATTLE
YOU SPILLED SO MUCH ...
YOU'RE LIKE A KID.

SHK
Just look! Oh, you ...
WHA ?!

LATERAL SHUFFLE!
GO!!
Fweet!
Hah
BABAM
HUP
?
YEP, ALWAYS GOOD TO GET EXERCISE!
COME ON, AYUMI, WHY DON'T YOU GIVE IT A TRY? FEELS GOOD!
...
HAHAHA

THERE YOU GO ACTING WEIRD AGAIN!
YOU BETTER BE DONE BY THE TIME THE COFFEE IS READY.
Or you'll spill it again.

I CAN'T BELIEVE THIS! AYUMI OWNS ONE OF THOSE?!
DO ALL 25-YEAR-OLD WOMEN HAVE THEM?!
He's so weird ...
PSSSHHH
S-SHE WOULDN'T HAVE EVEN MORE ...
SNEAK

SHHHT

UNDER-WEAR ...
SPREAD
SNIFF
SNIFF

AH, JUST PLAIN OLD UNDER-WEAR.
PHEW
That's good.
FLOP
RUMMAGE
I MUST HAVE JUST BEEN SEEING THINGS.
Of course! Haha
HM?

HER ROYAL HIGH-NESS'S SECRET WINDOW ?!!

WHAT'S WRONG ?
HM? OH, NOTHING ... HAHA-HA
FWIP
STUFF
STUFF
Must hide this ...
HM ?
...
...
BANANA
EGGPLANT
CUCUMBER
WALNUTS

EGGPLANT
CUCUMBER
Wh- What is
produce doing in this drawer?
CUCUMBER

COULD IT BE ?!!!
SHIVER
SHIVER
Could she be doing this ?!
WHING
BANANA
WALNUT
WALNUT
COMBINE
合体

HERE'S YOUR COFFEE.
KLAK

DON'T SPILL THIS ONE, OKAY?
HM? IS SOME-THING WRONG?
You're cowering?
...

RYU ...

...

?!
WHAT'S WRONG? DID SOME-THING HAPPEN?

GRAB

SHAKE
HUH?
WHAT WENT DOWN WITH YOU
OVER THESE PAST SIX MONTHS?
SHAKE
GUSH
GUSH
GAAAAH!
WHAT MADE YOU CHANGE SO?!
LOOM
Wake up, Ayumi!
EEEK! STOP IT!
HUH?
WHAT...
Huh?
Huh?

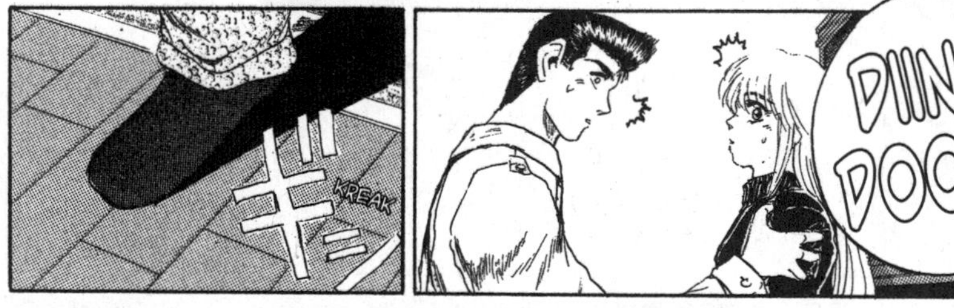
KREAK
DIING DOONG

HEY THERE, AYUMI.
RATTLE
OH, DAI!
WHAT?!
SPIN

TWITCH
COULD HE HAVE ...?!
Who's this guy?
IS HE THE ONE WHO CHANGED HER IN SIX MONTHS?!
CLENCH
TWITCH
HM?
YOU BASTARD!
YEEEK
SHAKE
WHAT DID YOU DO TO AYUMI?!
AAAH! WAIT, RYUJI!
WHAT'S WITH HIM?

SLAM
I'M HOME ♥
HUH?
OH!
PHEW! THE SHOOT TODAY WENT LONG.
RATTLE
WE DID A DOUBLE-HEADER SHOOT, SO— OH, A VISITOR?

YEAH. THIS IS RYUJI, A STUDENT FROM MY OLD SCHOOL.
OH!
Pretty cute!

THIS IS YOKO, ONE OF MY CLASSMATES FROM HIGH SCHOOL. THIS IS HER ROOM.
Howdy!
HUH?
SEE, I'M FREE-LOADING RIGHT NOW.
It's embarrassing, but...

FREE-LOADING?
WAIT?! SO, THIS ROOM IS...

HM? MY DRESSER...
HEY, KID, YOU OPENED THIS?

TUT-TUT! THIS IS FULL OF
MY PRECIOUS TOOLS.
RUMMAGE

HUP!
SWOOP
WHUMP
?!

WHISK
VRRM
VRRM
ALL RIGHT!

FOUR ROPE BONDAGE SHOOTS BACK TO BACK.
MAKES ME GAG.

GOT ALL MY TOOLS.
GOTTA GO OFF TO MY NEXT SHOOT.
STAMP
SO SOON?

ALL RIGHT, THEN♡ TIME TO EARN SOME MONEY!
Come on let's go.
Muah!
Sure!
WHAT? ROPE? WHAT?

SHE'S AN ADULT ACTRESS.
WHAT?!
You mean the famous ?!
She's pretty popular. Do you know her? Reina Ohsato ...

TH-THEN THE THINGS INSIDE THAT DRESSER WERE...
YEAH

DID YOU ...
THINK THEY WERE ...
...

...
You didn't ...

OH NO, LOOK AT THE TIME! I NEED TO GET GOING ...
R-RYUJI !!
Don't be sly!

BUT REALLY, IT FELT LIKE NO TIME HAD PASSED AT ALL SINCE WE LAST TALKED.
IT MAKES ME REMEMBER OLD TIMES.
...
HA, HAHA ...!
See ya

WAIT —
TAKE THIS...

I CAN'T BRING MYSELF TO THROW IT OUT.
I WAS HOPING TO GIVE IT TO YOU ALL THIS TIME...
HM?
Open it
later.
WHAT ... IS THIS?
OH! DON'T OPEN IT RIGHT NOW!

HUH?
KREEK
B-BYE!

WHAT COULD IT BE?
バタン
SLAM
What is it?

...

WHAT THE HECK, LET'S TAKE A LOOK!
RIP RIP
AHAHAHA!
SHE THOUGHT I'D WAIT?!

<No.10>
?!

I CAN'T BRING MYSELF
TO THROW IT OUT...
...

I WAS HOPING TO GIVE IT TO YOU ALL THIS TIME...
...

FWUMP

...

SKRRR-BWOM
YEAH... OF COURSE.
WHAT WAS I GETTING MY HOPES UP FOR?
IT ALL ENDED SOME TIME AGO.
AND YET I...
THUD
HOW LAME OF YOU...

RYUJI.

GRAKT
BOM

CUT IT OUT, YOU GUYS!
YOU THINK RYUJI'S GOING TO LET YOU GET AWAY WITH THIS?!
BAM
THUD
GYA-HAHA!

HUH ?
STILL TALK-ING ABOUT HIM?
THUD
SLAP

KOFF ...

NO MATTER HOW MUCH YOU PRAY...
KOFF KOFF
YOUR PRECIOUS PRINCE ISN'T COMING TO SAVE YOU.

RIGHT NOW, IT LOOKS LIKE
HE DOESN'T HAVE THE TIME TO BOTHER WITH YOU.

W-WHY WOULD YOU SAY THAT ?

Aah!
STOMP
...
MESS THIS BROAD UP GOOD.
Keheheh...
HURRY, RYUJI...
QUICK...
COME SAVE ME, MY RYUJI!

# Chapter 200: MY SWEET HOME

HEY NOW, YOU BETTER QUIET DOWN!
GRAB
HELP ME, RYUJI !!
STOP !!
HEH. YOU STILL THINK HE'S GONNA SAVE YOU?
NOOO!
WHAT A STUPID WOMAN!
DON'T YOU KNOW WHAT YOUR MAN'S DOING RIGHT NOW?

He's meeting with another woman!
Not just that, they're in her room!
?!
DON'T LIE TO ME LIKE THAT!
THEN WHY DON'T YOU ASK HIM LATER?
YOU'VE BEEN TOSSED AWAY.
Poor girl!
WHAT AN EVIL BOY-FRIEND!
I'd take you, though.
THERE'S NO WAY ...
RYUJI WOULD NEVER ...!!
GRAB

You better just give up!
...
Haha haha!
THAT'S NOT TRUE... I KNOW HE'LL COME...
I BELIEVE IN HIM.
THESE ARE ALL LIES!
WHAM
TSK, THESE CLOTHES ARE HARD TO TAKE OFF.
Ke-heh
JUST CUT 'EM OFF, THEN!
DON'T MOVE !!
LICK
HURRY, RYUJI...
RYU-JIII !!

KRIK
HUH ?
HM ?
SHOOM
Gyaa-agh!
KRASH
POP
BRIP
KRAK
THUD
ULP
AREN'T YOU ...

KRAK
...
Aku-
tsu
?!

TWITCH
THIS WOMAN HAS NOTHING TO DO WITH IT.
RIGHT, JOEY?
WHAT DID YOU COME HERE TO DO, JUNYA?
YOU'RE THE ONE WHO'S GOT NOTHING TO DO WITH THIS.
OR IS IT THAT
YOU WANT TO BE MY PLAYMATE?
KLENCH
HEH...

I DON'T KNOW WHAT YOU'RE SO WORKED UP ABOUT.
WHY IS THE "ICEMAN" EVEN KASHIYA DOESN'T DARE TOUCH BOTHERING WITH HER?
WHO IS THIS WOMAN?

WELL, WE'VE DONE ENOUGH HERE, ANYWAY.

LET'S WITH-DRAW FOR TODAY.

WE'VE GOT ONE MORE PIECE OF "BUSINESS" TO TAKE CARE OF TONIGHT.
ZAK
KE-KE-KEH

ANYWAY, I DON'T HAVE TIME TO PLAY AROUND WITH YOU.

IF YOU GET IN MY WAY AGAIN
I MIGHT GO NUTS TOO.
...
...

...
SKRRR
BWOOO
...
JOEY'S GOT A DEATHWISH?
JOEY'S SCARED OF DYING WITHOUT FEELING A THING!
CUT THIS CRAP.
WHUM
YOU CAN DO IT, CAN'T YOU?
PLEASE, GIVE JOEY HIS PEACE!
TIMES LIKE THIS, IT'S BEST TO JUST BLAST THROUGH THE SEISHO BYPASS...
DAH, ENOUGH. IT'LL ONLY GET ME DOWN ...

HUH?
Y-YO!
RYU...
JI?
THWOOSH
REACH

...

HEH

PULL

FWOOOOM
SKRR

YOU SCARED OF GOING HOME ALONE?
HUH? WELL... Hahaha
WHAT ARE YOU TALKING ABOUT, MAN?

WELL, STUFF HAPPENED, AND...
"STUFF"?

COULD YOU NOT TALK ABOUT THAT ANY-MORE?
HUH?

YOU WEREN'T PLAYING AROUND WITH ANOTHER WOMAN, WERE YOU?
TWITCH
O-OF COURSE NOT! I'D NEVER DO THAT! HAHAHA
Are you from Night Head?

I'M NOT MESSING AROUND WITH JOEY ANY-MORE.
YEAH, HE'D GIVE UP THEN.

BUT MAN, THAT WAS SOME-THING CRAZY.

I'M TALKING ABOUT JOEY!
I MEAN, HE WAS LIKE A MONSTER...

HEY?
THIS IS OUR TV...
HRN?

STAMP
?!
!
WH- WHAT THE HELL?!

Nagi-saaa?!

HEY! WAKE UP, NAGISA!
TH- THIS IS AWFUL! WHO WOULD...
!

?!

Aku-tsu?!


BRACE

TWITCH
TWITCH
YOU ...

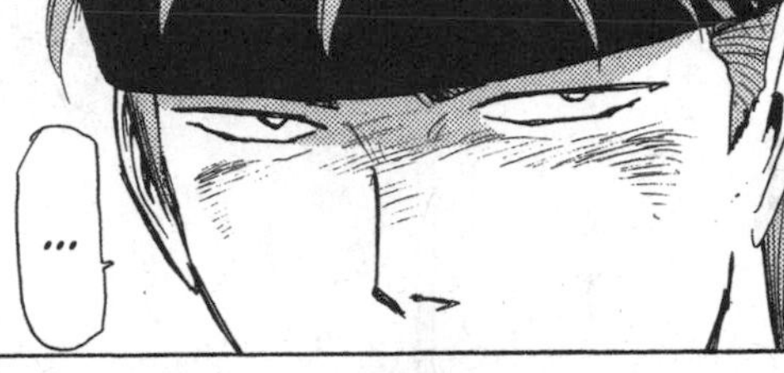
WHY ARE YOU HERE?
...
WHAT ARE YOU UP TO?

GRAB
WHO DID THIS? WAS IT YOU?!
SLAM
HUH?!

HEH
AS CLUELESS AS ALWAYS, I SEE.

STEP

HEY, WAIT! WE'RE NOT DONE TALKING YET!
AND YOU?

WHAT WERE YOU UP TO?

...
LEAVING YOUR WOMAN ON HER OWN THROUGH THIS?

IF YOU CARE ABOUT HER...
DON'T TRY TO GET RE-VENGE LIKE AN IDIOT.

HEY, WAIT!
AKUTSU!
FWOOOM
WHAT DO YOU MEAN BY THAT? HEY!
...
SKRRRR

IT'S FINE...

TWITCH
HE'S RIGHT.
...
IF I WAS HERE, THEN NAGI-SA...
TWITCH

DAM-
MIT,
WHO
DID
THIS
?!
I
WON'T
FOR-
GIVE
THEM
!
I'M
GONNA
HUNT
THEM
DOWN
AND
KILL
...

GRASP

YOU
CAME
BACK
...
PHEW
...

NAGISA
...

YOU
DON'T
NEED TO
GET RE-
VENGE.
JUST
DON'T
LEAVE
AGAIN.

STAY WITH ME.
I WON'T GO...
I WON'T GO ANY-WHERE ANY-MORE!
HUG

I'LL NEVER LEAVE YOU ALONE AGAIN!
NAGI-SAA !!
...

...

...

RISE

LISTEN UP! THE FLAME DANCERS WILL BE RIDING ROUTE 130 TONIGHT!
GWOOM
STAY TOUGH AND DON'T TAKE ANY CRAP FROM ANY-ONE!
YEAH!
FWOOOM
SKRRR

FWOOOOM
Grip

?!
THAT GUY FROM THE OTHER DAY...

FWOM
...

YOKO, I'M TAKING A DIF-FERENT ROUTE TO-NIGHT.
HUH?

Grip
COME WITH ME.
POW
POW

WE'RE FOLLOW-ING THAT GUY.
SOME-THING'S UP TONIGHT.

YEAH, HELLO?
ガレージ 佐藤
SATO'S GARAGE
OH, EIKICHI.

WHAT'S UP?

HUH?

OKAY, GOT IT.
SO WHERE SHOULD I GO?
KLICK

GREE

NO DOUBT ...
SOMETHING'S GOING DOWN.
BWOOM
SKRRR

ARE YOU SURE? IT'S THE GENERAL MEETING. WITH NO LEADER ...
THEN YOU GO, KATSUMI.
You're my second.
VRM
SOMETHING A HUNDRED TIMES MORE INTERESTING THAN
BA-BAM
A GENERAL MEETING SEEMS TO BE GOING ON.
TO-NIGHT
BOOM
BOOM
O,reason the need! r basest ggars Are in the poo st thing su perfluous!
follow me! le t you down a
Club
GTO The Early Years
Chapter 201: SEISHO SPEED KING 1

AIN'T
A NIGHT TO MISS.
BOOM

WHERE'S MY "BUTTER-FLY"?
Get me my pipe!
...
Wanna do some coke?
You got some?
Coke? Yesss!
Oh, sup.
HEARD YOU BROKE INTO DANMA'S PLACE, JOEY.
Yo
HEH. JUST LIKE ALWAYS, WORD GETS AROUND TO YOU FAST.
I'M THINKING ABOUT...
GOING TO GET DANMA'S OTHER GIRL NOW.
Fight, we kno w alon
I'M AT THE END OF MY TETHER.
...
Seems like my batteries are
about to run out at last, too.
Ke-ke-keh
SO YOU'RE...
GOING AT IT WITH DANMA?
...
SAY, KASHI-YA.

I'M NOT DOING THIS FOR YOU.
THIS IS ABOUT ME.
I KNOW WHAT'S UP, KASHI-YA.
I KNOW WHY YOU WANT ME TO KILL ONIZUKA.
SORRY, BUT I DON'T CARE WHO.
IT DOESN'T HAVE TO BE HIM. DANMA'D BE FINE.
JUST AS LONG AS THEY'D STAKE THEIR LIVES
ON KILLING ME.
CLUNK
THAT'S HOW I'LL ATONE ...
FOR her.
RATTLE

DASH
!
shink
?!
WHA ?
THUD
...
GRIP
YANK

HAH
Bro-ther?!
HAH
HAH
SHIK
HAH
HAH
UAAAA-AAGH!
WHAT THE HELL ARE YOU DOING?!
LET ME GO! DON'T YOU BUTT IN!
...
GRAB
I'LL BE THE ONE TO KILL HIM!
I'M GOING TO PUT HIM AT EASE!
...
I'LL SET YOU FREE WITH MY OWN HANDS, JOEY!
FREE FROM THE PAINLESS HELL YOU LIVE IN!
I DON'T WANT TO SEE YOU
Ass-hole...
FALL ANY MORE THAN THIS!
YOU DON'T GET IT, MAN.
YES I DO!

YOU'RE SCARED, RIGHT?! THAT ALL OF A SUDDEN, WITHOUT FEELING A THING,
DRIP
DRIP
...
YOU'D JUST DIE LIKE YOUR BATTERIES RAN OUT!
I'M YOUR OLDER BROTHER! OF COURSE I UNDERSTA—
IS THAT IT?
WHAT?
IS THAT ALL
THAT I SUFFER FROM?
ME, SCARED?
JOEY!
DON'T MAKE ME LAUGH.
SHK
?!
THUK
BSSHT
THIS KIND OF SUFFERING...
S-STOP IT, JOEY!
THUK
WH...
IS JUST ATONEMENT.
?!

I CAN'T ALLOW MYSELF TO DIE
WITHOUT FEELING PAIN OR SUFFER-ING.
I HAVE TO DIE WRITH-ING
SCREAMING IN AGONY THAT I DON'T WANT TO DIE.
IF I DON'T ...
I WON'T BE ABLE TO GO WHERE YOKO WENT.
WHAT ?
JOEY! ONI-ZUKA'S ...
BAM
ONI-ZUKA'S HERE!
TWITCH

ONI-ZUKA ?!
GRIN
!
I see
my escort is here.
HEY, WAIT! JOEY!
Hold...
SHUT UP, OLD MAN.

THUNDER ROADHOUSE
CAFE
EN

HEH
I'VE BEEN WAIT-ING FOR YOU
ZASH
...
ONI-ZUKA.

ALL THIS TIME, FOR YOU TO COME.

THE THOUGHT OF PICK-ING UP WHERE WE LEFT OFF
GIVES ME THE SHIVERS, ONI-ZUKA.
DO YOU WANT TO DIE THAT BADLY?
I'D BE HAPPY TO TEACH YOU.
...
THIS TIME YOU'LL SHOW ME, WON'T YOU?
DRIP
DRIP
THE STAIRWAY TO HEAVEN?

About just how scary
dying is.
Scary?
HAHA-HA!
ME, WHO DOESN'T FEEL PAIN? SCARED OF DEATH?
SOUNDS LIKE FUN.
TEACH ME, THEN.
TWITCH
SICILIAN ROULETTE ONE MORE TIME?
Ke-keh
OR DO WE CUT EACH OTHER WITH KNIVES?
Kekeh
NOT LIKE THAT.

KNG
KNG
KNG
WITH
BIKES
KAWASAKI
MID·KNIGHT
鬼
鬼
?!
Speed King.
A drag race!

HEY, SAYA.
YEAH
IT'S GETTING PRETTY CRAZY, HUH?
WE'LL BLOCK OFF THE ENTRANCE TO THE SEISHO BYPASS.
THEN WE START.
WE OPEN UP THE THROTTLE, THEN HOLD IT THERE.
THE FIRST ONE TO GET TO THE ODAWARA EXIT WINS.
KE-KE-KEH
IS THAT IT? WE JUST RIDE BIKES?
THAT'S MERE CHILD'S PLAY, ISN'T IT?
HOW ABOUT IT?
...
ARE YOU ON?
WELL, FINE. I'LL TAKE YOU UP. BUT—
IF YOU LOSE ...
I'M GONNA RIDE THAT BIKE OVER YOUR LEGS
SO YOU WON'T BE ABLE TO STAND AGAIN.
...
WHY NOT.
ALL RIGHT, IT'S DECIDED!

HEY, KASHIYA! YOU'VE GOT A NICE BIKE, DON'T YOU?
LEND ME THAT MONSTER.

ZZR-1100 TURBO.
THAT THING WILL DO 185MPH IF YOU'VE GOT THE BALLS FOR IT, RIGHT?

WHAT? KASHI-YA'S —

YOU DON'T MEAN HIS CUSTOM...

A ZZR-1100 TURBO ?!
WOAH! THAT MONSTER OF A MACHINE? THAT THING DOES 300 HORSES EASY!
This rocks !

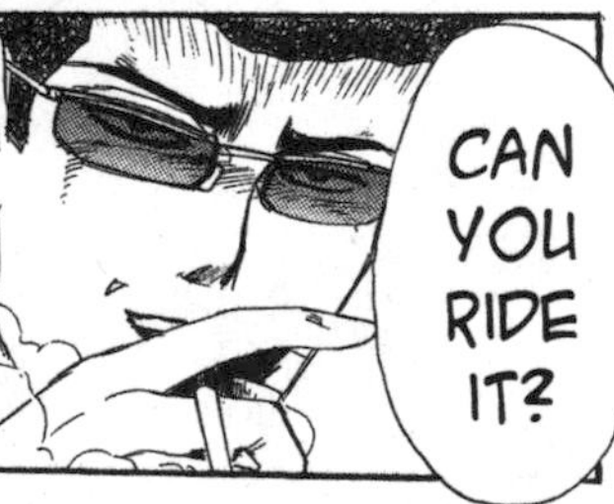
CAN YOU RIDE IT?
OVER-SIZED PISTONS AND ALL?

THERE'S NO WAY YOU CAN BEAT A WORLD-CLASS BEAST OF A MACHINE

...

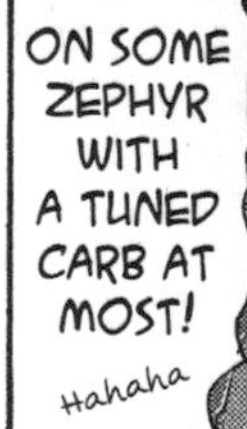
ON SOME ZEPHYR WITH A TUNED CARB AT MOST!
Hahaha

IT'S ONLY A BIKE.

SO, WHAT'LL YOU DO, ONI-ZUKA?
YOU DON'T STAND A CHANCE!

WHERE DID YOU GET THAT IDEA?

Who said anything about
going at it with this Zephyr 1100?
WHAT?
SO YOU'VE GOT AN EVEN HIGHER-POWERED BIKE?
KEH, IS THERE ANY THAT CAN BEAT THE OVER-250-HORSEPOWER MONSTER?
...
EI-KICHI!
YO, MA-SA-MI.
SORRY, MAN! I'M WAY LATE, GOT STUCK IN TRAFFIC.
SKRR
SORRY YOU HAD TO BRING IT HERE.
BWOMMM
?!
HM?

A ZII ?!
DWOOM
GWOOM
DWOOM
DWOOM
GWOOM
KAWASAKI
A candy red

DWOOM
ZII ?!
H-HE MEANS TO TAKE ON A ZZR-1100 TURBO WITH AN OUTMODED MACHINE?
GIVE IT A BREAK, THERE'D BE NO RACE!
...
!
IS THAT ZII...
WHAT'S WRONG, JOEY?
SCARED?
What the hell do you take me for?!

HONK
HONK
BEEEP

BEEEP
WHAT IN THE WORLD IS GOING ON WITH THIS TRAFFIC?
MOVE FOR-WARD!!
BEEEP
HOOONK

Beep Beeep
HEY, MOVE!!
Beeep
WHAT THE HELL ARE YOU DOING?

Honk Hooonk
Hooo-onk
Bee-eep
GRIN
...
Road's stop-ped!
Grin
Ka-hah
GRIN
SEISHO BYPASS: ROAD CLOSED

A ZII AND A ZZR 1100 TURBO IN A RACE?!
西湘バイパス
SEISHO BAIPASU
LOOKS LIKE IT'S BETWEEN JOEY AND SOME KID FROM SHONAN.
I HEAR THAT KASHIYA'S ZZR IS A BEAST. IT PUTS OUT OVER 300 HORSES.
My RZ is like, 40 horse-power!

## Chapter 202: SEISHO SPEED KING 2

300 HORSE-POWER?! IS HE INSANE? HE'D RACE IT WITH A ZII?!!
There's no way he can win!
That's the thing, though. It's not any ZII ...
It's *that* one.
HUH ?

BWOM
BWOM
BWOM
SHWINN
PSHH

HEY, THAT CAR THERE, STAY OUT!
We'll crush it!
GRRRRRMMM
KEEP AN EYE OUT SO THE COPS DON'T GET TO THE START LINE.
BWOMMMM
SOME-ONE TAKE A PHONE TO 134!
Bwo-mm
Fwom fwom
WOW, SAYA!
THIS IS A REAL PARTY.
Skr-rrr
THAT ONIZUKA GUY ...
JUST WHO IS HE?
How do you know him?
TAKING THE OLD CHAM-PION ZII
INTO A "SPEED KING" AGAINST A ZZR 1100?
...

HEH
Gwom Gwom
Fwom
Fwom
A ZII, HUH ...
SEEMS LIKE HE ISN'T
JUST SOME PERV.
AND... I'VE SEEN THAT ZII BEFORE.
I'M PRETTY SURE THAT'S ...

WOAH, THE BOOST ON THIS WASTE-GATE IS AWESOME!
BWOM
...
HOW MUCH DID YOU SPLURGE ON THIS, KASHI-YA?

FWO-MMM
AT ANY RATE, WHY'D THIS ONI-ZUKA
PICK SUCH AN OLD BIKE?
...
OMMM

IT WAS THE FASTEST AROUND.
HUH?

ONCE UPON A TIME, THAT ZII OWNED
THE TITLE OF "FASTEST" HERE IN KANA-GAWA.
FAST-EST?

THAT MACHINE BELONGS TO THE SPEED KING
LEGEND, KYOSUKE MASAKI.

WHAT?
THE MASAKI WHO'S BECOME A LEGEND?!

B-BUT WHY WOULD HE HAVE THAT BIKE?
...
Could he be ...?

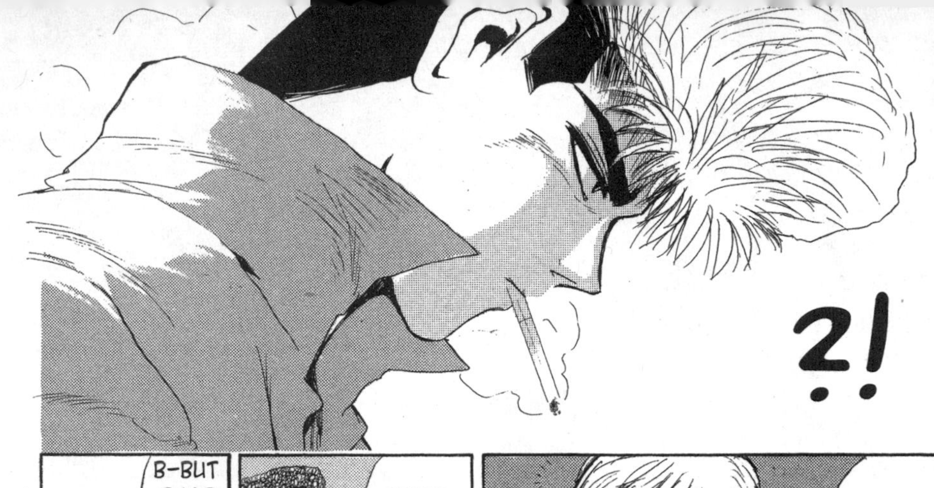
?!

AND WHAT ABOUT IT?
Hm?
MY "FIRE DEMON" IS A MONSTER. IT HASN'T TASTED DEFEAT ON THIS COAST A SINGLE TIME IN ITS LIFE.

THAT VINTAGE BIKE DOESN'T STAND A CHANCE.

B-BUT THAT ZII IS THE BIKE THAT LEFT
KASHIYA IN THE DUST BACK WHEN HE WAS ON HIS CB...

Twitch

WHAT?! KASHIYA HAS RACED THAT ZII BEFORE?

LEFT IN THE DUST?

Twitch
Me ??
Say that one more time.

EEK!
I'm sorry!
KA-SHI-YA ?!
JOLT

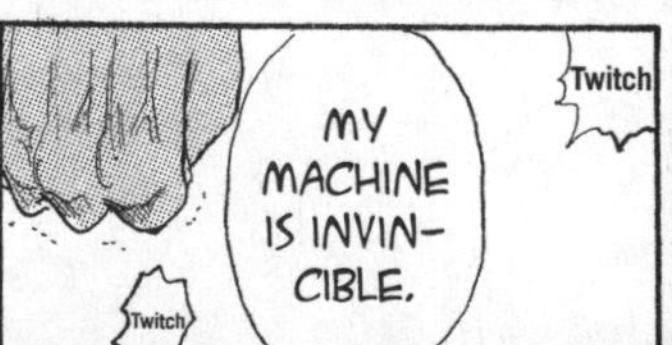
Twitch
...
MY MACHINE IS INVINCIBLE.
Twitch

BWOM
...
BWOM
There's no way it'd lose
to that Shonan punk.
Vsshhhhh
Bshhh
BWOM
WHAT ARE YOU GUYS GOING ON ABOUT?
WHO CARES ABOUT HOW THEY PERFORM. I'M THE ONE ON IT, AND I WON'T LOSE,
NOT TO THAT BLUFFING LITTLE PUNK.
JUST WAIT AND SEE.
Shhhhhh
I'LL TAKE HIM OUT WITHOUT A SWEAT.
Bsh-hhh
MAKE ME SCARED OF DYING?
That kid?
DON'T MAKE ME LAUGH.
Bshh-rrrr
BWOM
I'LL TEACH HIM INSTEAD
TRUE FEAR OF DEATH.
BWOM
Bshh-rrrr

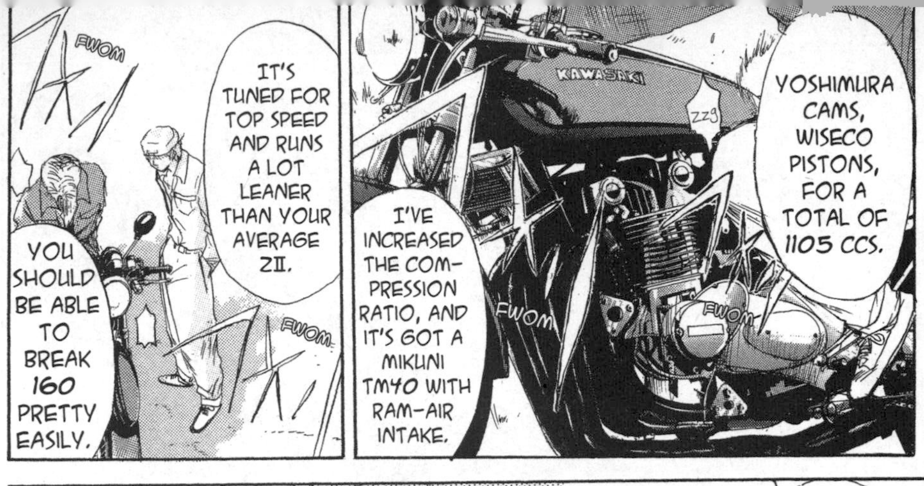
YOSHIMURA CAMS, WISECO PISTONS, FOR A TOTAL OF 1105 CCS.
KAWASAKI
ZZG
FWOM
FWOM
I'VE INCREASED THE COMPRESSION RATIO, AND IT'S GOT A MIKUNI TM40 WITH RAM-AIR INTAKE.
IT'S TUNED FOR TOP SPEED AND RUNS A LOT LEANER THAN YOUR AVERAGE ZII.
FWOM
FWOM
YOU SHOULD BE ABLE TO BREAK 160 PRETTY EASILY.

STILL, OLD IS OLD.
ITS FORK AND FRAME ARE WOEFULLY OUTDATED.

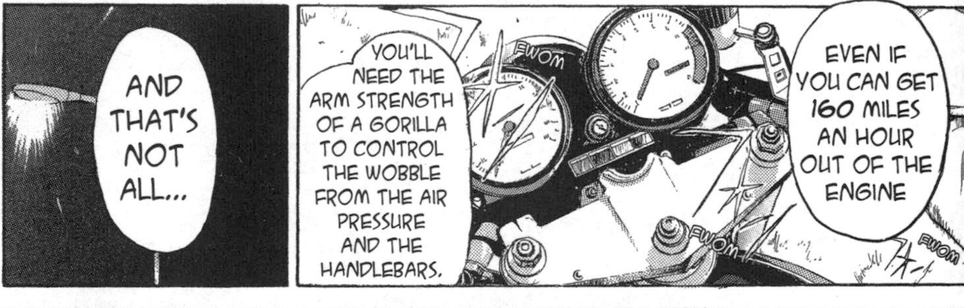
EVEN IF YOU CAN GET 160 MILES AN HOUR OUT OF THE ENGINE
FWOM
FWOM
FWOM
YOU'LL NEED THE ARM STRENGTH OF A GORILLA TO CONTROL THE WOBBLE FROM THE AIR PRESSURE AND THE HANDLEBARS.
AND THAT'S NOT ALL...

IT'S SET TO RUN EXTRA LEAN TO MASAKI'S TASTE.
...
FWOM
EVEN IF YOU CAN CONTROL THE JITTER
FWOM
AND DO GET 160 OUT OF THE ENGINE...

TEN MIN
when the critical expansion point is reached
IS THE MAX.

IF YOU KEEP THE THROTTLE OPEN ANY LONGER THAN THAT...

?!

THE ENGINE MIGHT BURN ITSELF OUT. IF THAT HAPPENS...
YOU'RE GONNA HIT THAT ASPHALT HARD AND FAST.
YOU STILL WANNA DO IT ?

You wanna get this thing
to take on that hunk of modern techno-logy?

DON'T WORRY... IT'LL BE FINE.

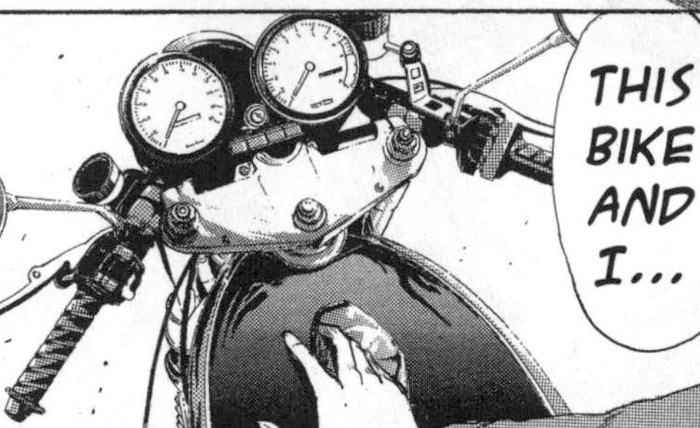
THIS BIKE AND I...

GET ALONG WELL.

I WON'T LOSE.

TSK

ZASH

YOU READY?! THE RACE STARTS FROM HERE.

YOU HAVE TO HOLD IT OPEN!
WHOEVER GETS TO THE FINISH LINE FIRST WINS!

OF COURSE, IF YOU CRASH OR IF THE COPS GRAB YOU ON THE WAY
THE RACE ENDS THERE.

WELL, IF YOU CRASH GOING OVER 150
YOU WON'T BE ABLE TO CONTINUE EVEN IF YOU WANTED.

THE FINISH LINE IS THE SEISHO EXIT!
GOT IT?

GCHK
BWOMM

DLIMM
BLIMM

FWOM
FWOM

GWOM
GWOM
GWOMM

THIS RACE ...
IS GOING DOWN
OOOOMMM
キュキュ
SKRRRR

IN HIS-TORY!!
WHAP
VWOOOOO
DSKRRRR

!
FWAAAAAAAAAM
THEY'RE ... NECK AND NECK?
HEH
WHIII ING
SNAP
BOOM
?!
THAT'S THE TURBO KICKING IN!
HA HA HA! WHAT'S WRONG, OLD CHAMP?!
WANT ME TO GIVE YOU A TOW?

I'll drag you to the gates of heaven!
Brm
KWM
Brm
DKRRR
KWM
ALL RIGHT, WE'RE GOING AFTER THEM!
DON'T FALL BE-HIND!
KA-SHI-YA.
HEH
...
THAT ZII BEING THE FASTEST IS JUST A FAIRY TALE TODAY.
Follow 'em!
Hey, let's go!
Du-Dum
Du-Dum
Dum
BIKES OF THAT LEVEL ARE A DIME A DOZEN NOW.
WE'RE NOT
IN THAT ERA!
FROM HERE ON OUT
IS MY ERA!

PING
ACK!
DMMMM

HAHAH! WHAT'S WRONG, ONIZUKA?!
FWO-MMM
BWO-MMM
YOU STARTING TO UNDERSTAND?!

A LEGEND DOESN'T AMOUNT TO MUCH
EXCEPT FOR NOSTALGIA!
GWOMMM

GET IT YET
ONI-ZU-KAA?!

GWOMMMM

HEY, DO YOU SEE THEM?
FWOM
FOOOM
THAT'S THEM, RIGHT? DAMN, ALREADY AT 125 MPH!
GWOMMMM

JOEY'S GOT MORE ROOM TO BREATHE, DOESN'T HE?!
His revs seem pretty low...
BUT DAMN, EVEN SO!
GWOOMMM
THE ZII MUST BE MAXED OUT!
The handlebars are shaking like crazy!
GWOM
JOEY'S GOT THIS ONE IN THE BAG!
Damn the wind pressure is crazy!
WHAT'S WRONG, ONIZUKA?!
WE'RE STILL ONLY AT 125 MPH!
Damn
BWOMMMM
FWOMMM
WEREN'T YOU GOING TO SHOW ME, ONIZUKA?
GWOOOMM
WITH THAT LEGEND OF A MACHINE?
THE FEAR OF DEATH?!
TIME TO GO SEE.
HUH?
BOOM

HUH?
Plip

ZKRRRRRRR

?!
WHA ?!
H-He pops a wheelie ...
REALLY?

GRAAAAA
KEEP UP WITH ME
ON THAT GIMMICK LUMP OF METAL.
Bastard!!
at 125 mph ?!!

GRRRRRMM
A wheelie at 125 mph?!
SKR RRR
GTO The Early Years
Chapter 203: SEISHO SPEED KING 3

SO, THAT ZII'S SET TO RUN PRETTY LEAN.

I SEE, HE RAN HIS BIG MOUTH ABOUT TEACHING ME THE FEAR OF DEATH

Fuck this ...
PLAY-TIME'S OVER.
Chik
Chik
I DON'T BELIEVE
IN LEG-ENDS.
And I can't stand anyone who does!
KREEEN
FWOM
That can't be! How could a ZII have so much power?!
BECAUSE HE HAD ACCESS TO THAT LEGENDARY MACHINE.
GRIP
HM?

BOOM
Kawasaki
WOAH! WHAT IS THAT?!
GWOMMM
DAMN, I CAN'T KEEP UP ANYMORE!
WE'VE MAXED OUT!
How fast is he going?!
HA HA HA HA! LET'S SEE HOW LONG

KRRR
PSHHHHHHHH
SKR-
SKRRR
?!

KRRRR
BRRT
BRRT
piss
drib-
ble

A B-
BIKE?!

YOU LAST IN THIS WIND PRESSURE ON A BIKE WITH NO FAIRING !

SAYA!!
Fwaaam
Shwom
POP
Fwom
DID YOU SEE THAT JUST NOW?!
I CAN'T BELIEVE HOW THAT MONSTER JUST ACCELERATED!
THERE'S REALLY NO WAY THAT A ZII CAN KEEP UP!
GWOOMMM
UH-UH, THAT'S NOT IT.
...
DO YOU GET IT NOW? IT'S ABOUT POWER!
GWOOMMMM
MAYBE ON A MOUNTAIN ROAD, BUT IN A DRAG RACE, IT'S NO MATCH!

GLANCE

HUH, NOT EVEN A SIGN OF HIM.
THAT LITTLE SPURT OF EFFORT BACK THERE MUST HAVE BEEN THE LIMIT.

PFT, BORING!
GUESS I'LL SLOW DOWN AND PLAY AROUND WITH HIM...

GSHHT

?!
WOAH!
SKRRRR
SKRR
WHAT THE— WOBBLED ALL OF A SUDDEN.
DAMN!
WH-WHAT WAS THAT?!
A pebble?
IT FELT LIKE I HIT SOMETHING...
?!

Oni-
zuka
?!
GSHHT
SSST

ZOOM
?!
!
SKRR
BWOOM

KICK
Grrt

SKRRRR
SHIT!
Skr

GWOOOM
HAAH
HAAH
SH-SHIT ...
DON'T KID ME.
I'D NEVER LET YOU...
GRIP
GWOOO

HELL, TIME TO OPEN IT UP MORE ...
Krrm
TO OPEN IT UP ALL THE WAY!
Sshhh
GWOOOM
HOW ABOUT NOW?
Wip
CAN YOU STILL KEEP UP?!
Rr
THERE'S NO WAY YOU ...

WHY? HOW, ON THAT CLUNKER, DOES HE KEEP UP WITH ME?
オオオオオオ
GOOOOOO
BRT
BRT
Jsht
Jsht
NO MATTER HOW MUCH YOU TUNE AN OLD MODEL LIKE THAT, IT SHOULDN'T EVER BREAK 150!
Jsht
Shhg-woom
DOES HE HAVE NITROUS ON THAT THING?!
?!

GWOOOOM
THAT'S WHAT IT IS! HE'S RIDING IN MY SLIP-STREAM ...!!
Shhg-woom
SLIP-STREAM !!

I GOTTA SHAKE HIM OFF.
SHAKE HIM OFF.
Kng
THAT'S HOW HE'S REACHING THIS SPEED ON A ZII...
Kng

NOT TO HIM!
I CAN'T LOSE!
MORE... MORE ACCELERA-TION...
I NEED TO OPEN UP THE THROTTLE MORE...

WHIP

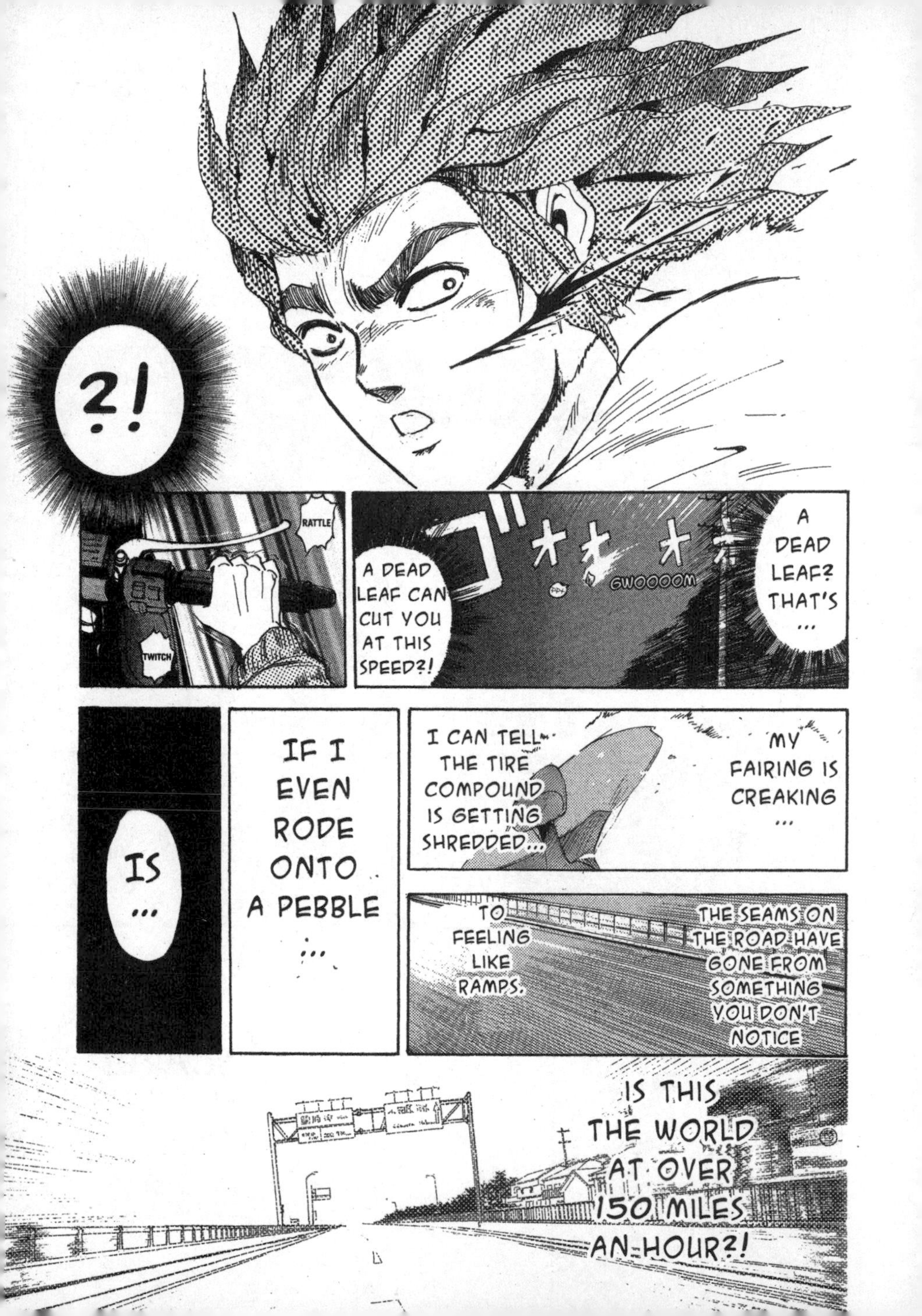
?!
A DEAD LEAF? THAT'S ...
A DEAD LEAF CAN CUT YOU AT THIS SPEED?!
GWOOOOM
RATTLE
TWITCH
MY FAIRING IS CREAKING ...
I CAN TELL THE TIRE COMPOUND IS GETTING SHREDDED...
THE SEAMS ON THE ROAD HAVE GONE FROM SOMETHING YOU DON'T NOTICE
TO FEELING LIKE RAMPS.
IF I EVEN RODE ONTO A PEBBLE ...
IS ...
IS THIS THE WORLD AT OVER 150 MILES AN HOUR?!

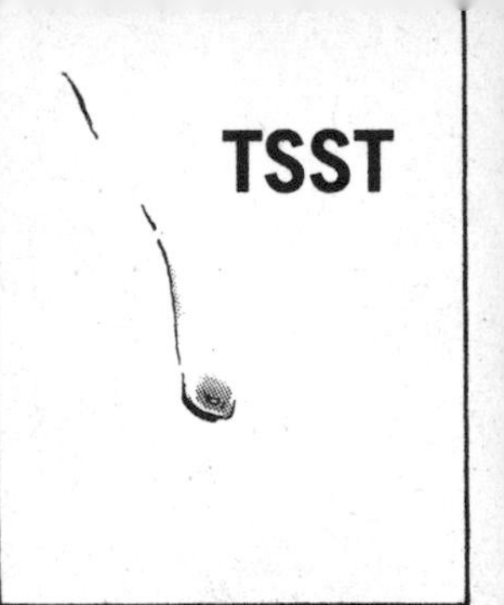
TSST

PTT

WHAT?
TSST

?!
PTT

SWEAT?!
I'M SWEATING?!
TSST
PTT

I'M BEING HIT BY ALL THIS COLD AIR
FWOOOOM
SH-RRR

AND I'M SWEATING?!

COULD I BE...

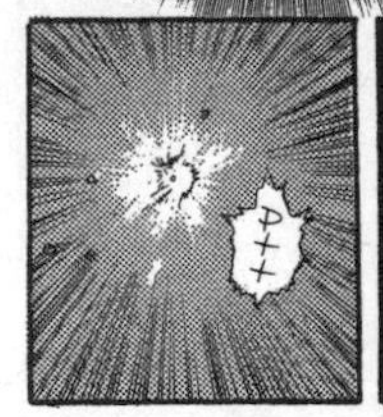
PTT

SCARED?

GWOOM
HEH. THERE'S NO WAY.
I'M ONLY FACING OFF AGAINST SOME PUNK FROM SHONAN.
KAWA

THERE'S NO WAY...
THERE'S NOTHING LEFT FOR ME TO LOSE.
YEAH, EVER SINCE THAT DAY...
EVER SINCE THEN, I...
JOEY ...
WE'RE ALIKE ...
YOU AND I...
PLINK
IT HURTS JOEY ...
PLEASE, SAVE ME...

PLEASE KILL ME...

WAAAAAGH!

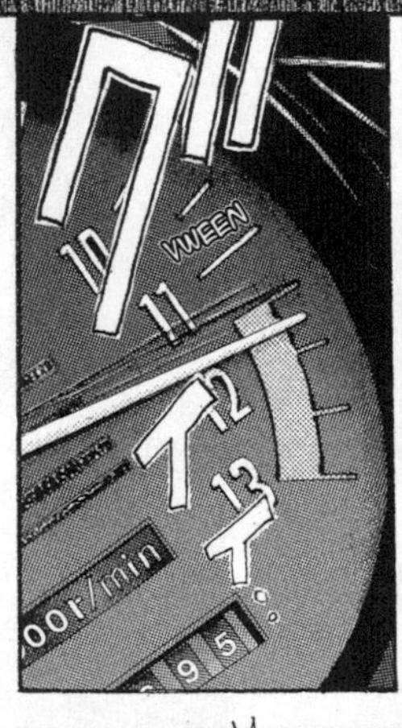
VWEEN
r/min

SHUNP
?!

SHWIP

THE WORLD ...
CHANGED ?
EVERY-THING IS JUST
RUSHING BY MY EYES.
ALL I CAN MAKE OUT IS ONE POINT IN THE DISTANCE...
IT'S LIKE I'M INSIDE A TUNNEL.
WHAT WOULD I BE IN FOR
IF I KEPT IT OPEN MORE THAN THIS?
160
170
260
280
SST

?!
WHA ?!
Come on.

I'll show you
what's on the other side of this tunnel!

GKKKT
THIS IS PURPLE CROWN.
BWOOOOM
DO YOU SEE THE ZZR AND THE ZII YET?
I'M AT THE KOZU REST AREA... NO SIGNS OF THEM YET. OVER.
SEND WORD ONCE YOU SEE THEM, OVER.

DAMMIT, WON'T THIS THING GO FASTER?!
I SHOULD HAVE CUT THE LIMITER IF IT WAS GOING TO ACT LIKE THIS.
KA-SHI-YA,
WHAT WILL YOU DO?

IF YOUR MACHINE LOSES...
BLUE ROSE COULD
FALL APART FOR REAL.
HEH
DON'T WORRY.
MY MACHINE IS THE FASTEST.
THERE'S NO WAY IT'LL LOSE TO A CLUNKER LIKE THAT.

IT'S HERE?!
The ZII!!
The ZII's in the lead!!
GTO The Early Years
Chapter 204: SEISHO SPEED KING 4

FWA-
AAA-
AAA
WHANNG
BOLT
WOAH! HOW FAST ARE THEY GOING ?!

CRACK
THE ZII ?
The ZII ...
is in the lead ??
Pop
PIP
BOLT
WHY ?!
WHY CAN'T I PASS HIM ?!
THERE'S NO WAY!
240
260
280
300
160
170
180
I-I'M DOING OVER 175!!
WHAT'S WITH THAT ?!

EVEN MY ZZR'S BODY...
IS BOWING THIS MUCH!

HOW, IN THIS WIND PRESSURE?
RIDICULOUS!

WE'RE GOING SO FAST A PEBBLE COULD SEND US FLYING!

DRIVING WITH TUNNEL VISION LIKE THIS
ON THAT OLD CHAMP?!!

Psh

WE'LL DIE...

THUMP
AT THIS RATE
THUMP
BOTH OF US, FOR REAL...

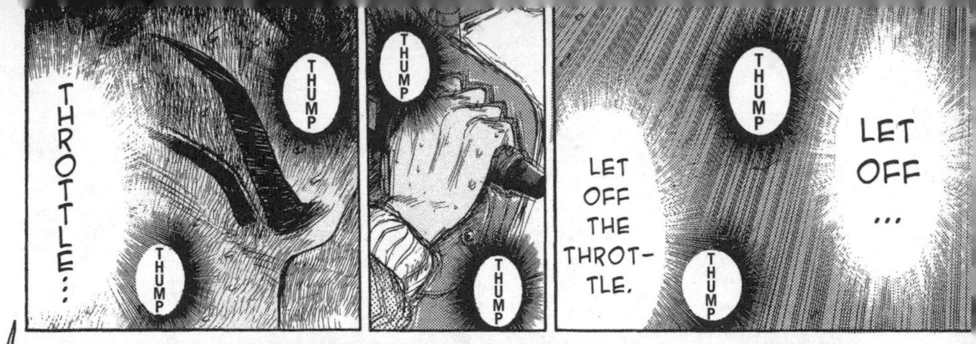

I LOVE YOU, JOEY...

BOOM
SHRRRRR
I CAN'T LOSE FOR
CRAP LIKE THIS !!
Shhhh
GRRMP

!

KREEEEE
NOT HERE
TO SOME PUNK ...

WHA ?!
WHANNG
Grrr rrm
H-HE'S PULLING AWAY FROM ME?! HOW?
I'M ALMOST AT 185 !!

HOW FAST ...
GWOOOM
IS THAT ZII GOING ?!!
GRT
?!

BOOM
SKR-RRR
UGH?!
AAAAGH!
Skrr
AGH!
THUMP
I...
I'M SCARED!!
THUMP

THUMP
I CAN'T BUDGE!!
THUMP
NOT EVEN TO LET OFF THE THROT-TLE!

THUMP
HE'S READY TO DIE...
THUMP
BRT
280
300
NO... HE'S THE REAP-ER!!
BRT
AND HE'S COME TO TAKE ME!!
URAAAAAA
AAAAAGH!
KEIHIN

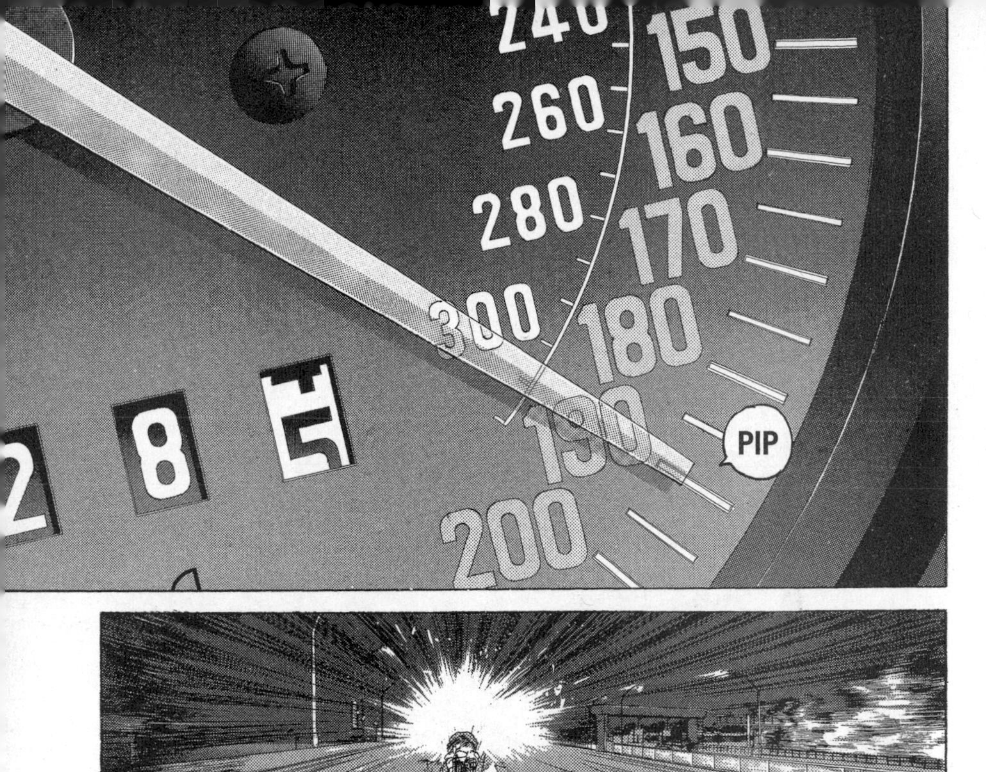
PIP

WHAT?

LIGHT...
I'M STEEPED IN PURE WHITE LIGHT?


I CAN'T SEE ANYTHING...
I CAN'T HEAR ANYTHING...

WHAT HAPPENED?
AREN'T I IN SEISHO?


160
170
180
280
300
9
7

ONIZUKA?

H-HEY, WAIT!
WHERE ARE YOU...

THAT'S IT, NOW I REMEMBER ...

THIS WHITE LIGHT ...
JUST LIKE BACK THEN ...

YEAH, THAT TIME ...
WHEN I CRASHED ON MY BROTHER'S R1-Z.
IT WAS LIKE THIS.

DID I JUST...

DIE?

SNAP

HEY, HOW ABOUT THE TWO OF US...
JUST RUN AWAY FROM THIS HOSPITAL?

I MEAN, YOU ALWAYS LOOK SO SAD.
I KNOW.
BECAUSE I FEEL THE SAME WAY.

I'LL STAY WITH YOU.

BE BY
YOUR SIDE.
AL-WAYS...
YOKO...
YOKO, IS THAT YOU?
YOKO?
NO! IT'S A DREAM!

DREAM
YEAH, THIS PLACE MUST BE...

SNAP
IT HURTS!
JOEY !!

SHATTER

IT HURTS SO BAD ...

Plip
Plip
OEY ...

HOLD ON, YOKO!

JOEY
YOKO !
I OVE OU ...

I LOVE YOU SO MUCH ...

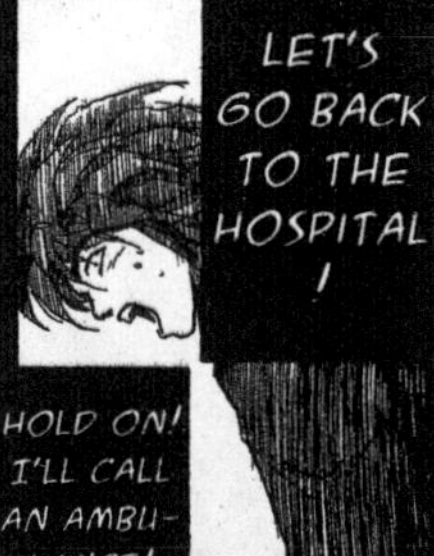
LET'S GO BACK TO THE HOSPITAL !
HOLD ON! I'LL CALL AN AMBU-LANCE!

IT'S OKAY.

I KNOW... MEDICINE CAN'T HELP ME NOW.
TUG

JUST LET ME DIE... AT YOUR HANDS, YES?
I WANT TO GO HELD BY THEM.

YOKO?

GKOFF
YOKO, HEY! HOLD ON!!

Goff
YOKO!
Koff
PLEASE, HURRY...

JOEY?
I CAN'T DO IT.
I COULD NEVER ...
PLEASE
HURRY
JOEY
I'LL NEVER
EVER FORGET YOU...
YOO KOO-OOO!
mph
180
320
190

WHAM

?!
A BIKE
...
IS FLY-ING ??!

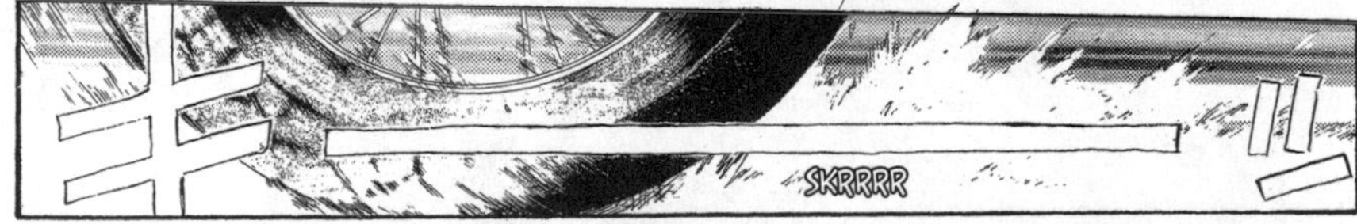
SKRRRR

SKREEEE
GWOOOM

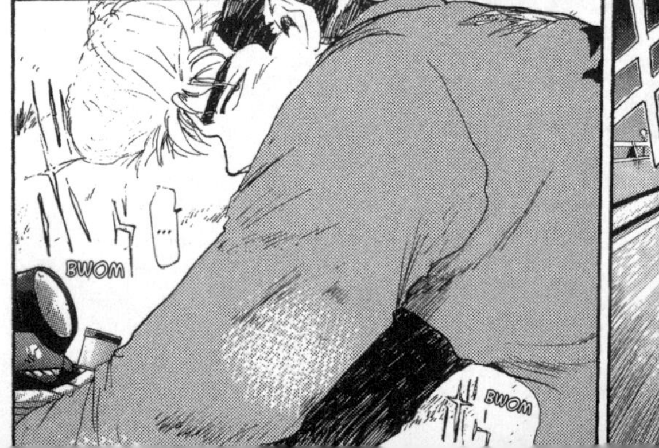
...
BWOM
BWOM

GTO The Early Years
Chapter 205:
SEISHO SPEED KING 5

STARS

LOOK, YOKO, STARS...

NOW I CAN FINALLY COME,

NO, JOEY.

JOEY, REMEM-BER...
YOKO ...

THE ONE WHO
TRULY LOVES YOU.
WHAT ?
WHAT ARE YOU SAYING?

I LOVE YOU ...
JOEY.
I'LL NEVER FORGET YOU.
SO PLEASE ...
REMEMBER ...
YOU'RE MY ONLY ...

YOKO
...
HEY... WHERE ARE YOU GOING?
YOKO
...

HE'S COME TO...

ONI-ZUKA ...

DID YOU ...

IDIOT

IT WAS YOUR BRO.

YOUR OLDER BROTH-ER
SAW YOU FLUNG INTO THE SEA AND DIVED IN.

HE MUST BE NUTS TO JUMP INTO THE COLD NOVEMBER WATER.
...

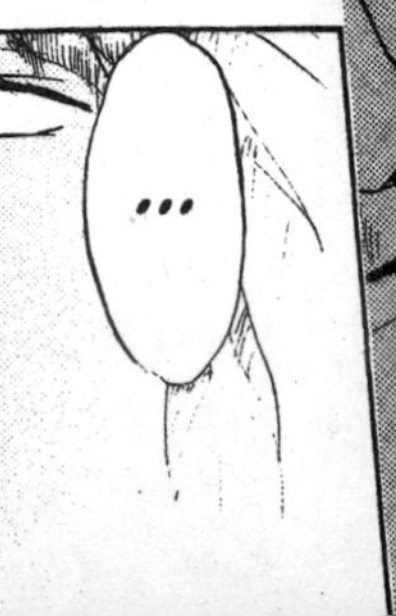
...

I MET YOKO.

IN THE SKY ...
HEH ...
YOU SHOULD ...
THANK YOUR BROTH-ER.
HEY, ONI-ZUKA.
WAS THAT JUST A DREAM ?
I SAW NOTHING BUT LIGHT
ONCE WE BROKE 185 MPH.
I'M SURE THAT I...
...
WHO KNOWS.

JOEY!!
FWAM
BROTHER?
I SEE ...
PLIP
I GET IT, YOKO ...

WHAT A BEAU-TIFUL NIGHT ...
HUH, BRO?

JOEY.
YOU ...
SORRY, ONI-ZUKA.
I CAUSED YOU A LOTTA TROU-BLE.

I'M SET
ON LIVING.
JOEY...

I DON'T KNOW HOW MUCH LONGER I CAN
BUT I'LL GO BACK TO THE HOSPITAL FOR NOW.

ONI-ZUKA ...
SOME DAY ...

SOME DAY, IF I LEAVE THE HOS-PITAL
STILL ALIVE ...

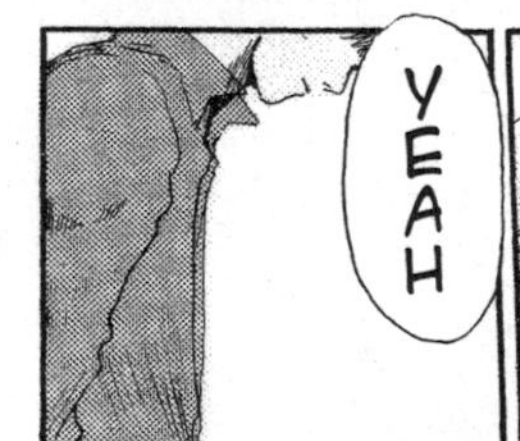
YEAH

WHEN YOU DO...

LET'S SETTLE THIS
WITH OUR FISTS.
YUP
KOFF
JOEY! HOLD ON!
TO THE HOSPITAL, NOW!
...
...

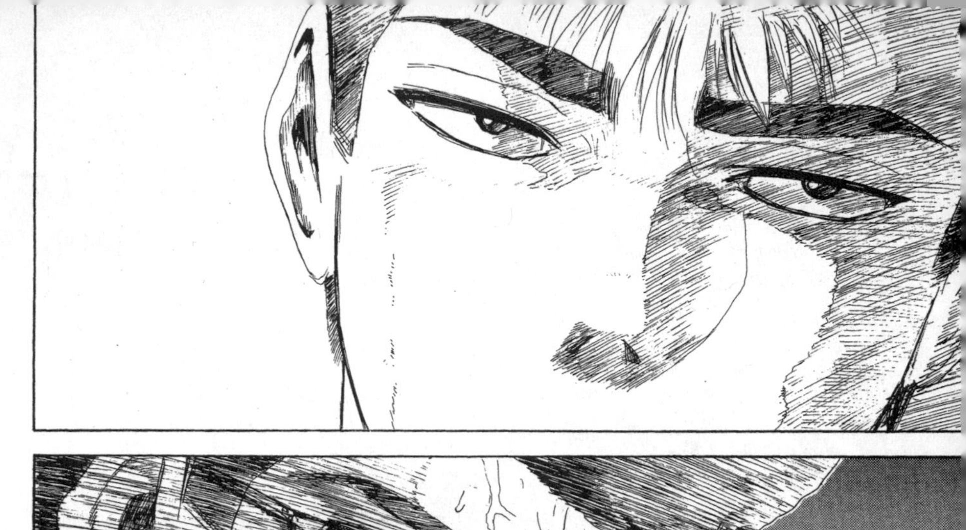

GRIP
爆
鬼

スッ
SHOOM
HEH
SO, YOU LOSE THIS ONE?
KASHI-YA...
...
SO HE'S THE ONE MASAKI DUG.

GET OUT OF THE WAY!
I SAID MOVE!
ONI-ZUKA!
YOU...
You won?
HOW?
with that clunker?!
PAT
SAY, WANT TO
GO GET A DRINK?
Hm?
Y-YOU IDIOT! TELL ME ...
HOW FAST DID YOU END UP GOING?!
DID YOU SERIOUSLY BREAK 185 MPH ON THAT ZII?!

SO WHAT
IF I DID.
...

C'MON, LET'S GO!
WHAT, "SO WHAT"?
TAKE THAT ARM OFF MY SHOULDER!
HEY !!

YO, THAT BATTLE IN SEISHO YESTER-DAY?
YOU MEAN THAT SPEED TRIAL?
THEY SAY THE ZII DID OVER 185 MPH.
S-SERIOUSLY? THAT OLD MODEL CAN GO THAT FAST?
LOOKS LIKE IT LEFT A 300-HP ZZR IN THE DUST.
Already legendary!
I CAN'T BELIEVE IT.
WHO WAS ON IT?
ISN'T IT OBVIOUS, YOU IDIOT?
ONLY ONE GUY IN SHONAN WOULD BE THAT CRAZY.
Oh, of course!
'MORNING, SIR!
Mister Onizuka!
Morning!

YO
STEP
GTO The Early Years
Chapter 206:
EGG CLUB, CHICK CLUB

ROLL
DID YOU REALLY BATTLE ON SEISHO ?!
STOMP
STOMP

MAN, THAT'S AWE-SOME!
How'dya get a ZII to do 185??
I don't really know, either!
DAMMIT, WHY DIDN'T YOU LET ME KNOW ?
WHOO

YUP.

I CAN'T BELIEVE I MISSED SUCH A HISTORIC RACE!
I hadn't a clue!
IT'S ALREADY THE TALK AROUND TOWN!

REALLY? SO IT'S ALREADY GETTING THAT BIG?
Even the girls?
OF COURSE IT IS!
They won't stop screeching about it!

YOU TOOK OUT THAT JUNKIE AND THAT CIGARETTE-SMOKING BASTARD!
I BET EVEN NAKAJO FROM ENO COMMERCIAL MUST BE UPSET!
Ya think ?

AFTER THIS, YOKOSUKA'S BASICALLY OURS.
AT THIS RATE, WE CAN SWEEP THROUGH AND CONQUER ALL OF KANAGAWA!! SHALL WE?
I'll help out!
WE'LL SLAM THROUGH AND RAISE THE ONI-BAKU FLAG!
HA HA HA HA!
RAISE THE FLAG!!
LET'S DO IT!!

UGH, THIS IS SO STUPID.
CONQUER KANAGAWA? ARE YOU ALL IDIOTS?
WHY ARE YOU GETTING SO EXCITED OVER WINNING A LITTLE BIKE RACE?
Ugh
HMM, WHAT DO WE HAVE HERE? OH, SAEJIMA! WE HAVEN'T SEEN MUCH OF YOU RECENTLY ...
YOU'RE NOT JEALOUS, ARE YOU?
Pft

I CAN SEE WHY. I MEAN, THE "MAD DOG OF KAMAKURA"
...
HAS RECENTLY JUST BEEN THE COMIC RELIEF!
I'll kill you, punk.
TWITCH
STRETCH
MAYBE YOU'VE GONE AS FAR AS YOU CAN GO WITH THIS SCARY FACE OF YOURS!
...
YOU CAN'T JUST BE ALL SHOW, YOU KNOW!
SQUISH
MAYBE YOU SHOULD BECOME ONE OF MY UNDERLINGS WHILE YOU STILL CAN!
...
HMMMM?
OR ARE YOU GOING TO TEAM UP WITH THAT BIG HULK KIWAMEZAWA AND TRY TO CONQUER THE WORLD?
Pf-ff+
BLUB
Pf+
Like some bad guys!!
...
SNAP
TWITCH
TWITCH

WHAT'RE YOU TRYING TO LOOK TOUGH FOR?
SLAP
SLAP
SNAP
YOU'RE LASSIE, THE MAD DOG OF KAMA-KURA!

I-I'LL KILL YOU DEAD, BAS-TARD!
THUD
Woah!

DON'T TRY TO RUN, YOU TURD!
OVER HERE, BOY!
...
Whee !!

WHY'S THAT IDIOT HIGH?
Whee
You're getting stabbed today!
LET HIM HAVE HIS FUN.

EVEN IN THE OTHER CLASSES, IT'S ALL THE TALK.
IT'S LIKE HE REALLY DID SOME-THING.

DID? HIM?
HEY, DON'T MAKE ME LAUGH HERE.

YOU THINK HE'S GOT WHAT IT TAKES
TO KEEP THAT FACADE ?
That perv?

JINGLE JINGLE
Benny's
Benny's

KLATT
HM?

SIRI!
ZAKK
ZAKK
ZAKK
HEH
YO

WHO IS HE?
YOU DON'T KNOW? THAT'S ONIZUKA FROM TSUJI HIGH! YOU KNOW, THE GUY WHO WON THE BATTLE IN SEISHO...
WHAT? HIM?!
THIS IS AMAZING, ONIZUKA! EVERY-ONE'S LOOKING THIS WAY!
MAN, YOU'RE MAKING ME BLUSH.
Haha!

E-EXCUSE ME, ARE YOU ONIZUKA, OF ONI-BAKU?
HUH? I GUESS SO.
Hm?
WOW! OH MY GOD! Y-YOU'RE THE REAL THING?! I'M A BIG FAN!
Oh yeah?
Ha ha!
I'M ONLY IN 8TH GRADE, BUT I WANT TO BE LIKE YOU ONE DAY...
UH, AS A SOUVENIR, COULD YOU GIVE ME A STARE-DOWN?
HUH?
GRIT
Like this?!
TH-THANK YOU V-VERY MUCH!!
Awesome!!
HAHAHA! IT'S NOTHING AT ALL!
...
...
Weird taste
WELCOME!
JINGLE

SHINE
SHINE
YO, EIKICHI ♡
SHINE
Hello!
OH, RYUJI!!
I HEARD YOU TOOK CARE OF HIM? That junkie?
MAN, YOU'RE REALLY SOME-THING!
Hi!
WE'VE BASICALLY TAKEN OVER YOKOSUKA THANKS TO THIS!
I DON'T DESERVE TO BE THE "BAKU" IN ONI-BAKU.
MAYBE I'M NOT MEANT FOR THE BAD BOY LIFE-STYLE!
I'M REALLY NO MATCH FOR YOU!
HA HA... WHAT'RE YOU SAYING? ONI-BAKU NEEDS YOU!
As the number 2!
Ha ha ha
Cut it out!

ANYWAY, WHAT HAVE YOU BEEN DOING? YOU HAVEN'T EVEN BEEN TO SCHOOL.
Why so shiny?
I HEAR YOU TWO WERE COOPED UP ALL THIS TIME.
HM?

WELL, THAT'S THE THING ♡
HM?
YEAH
WE WERE TOGETHER THE WHOLE TIME AFTER THAT JUNKIE MESSED UP OUR HOME...
IT JUST FLARED UP FOR US.

WE SHUT OURSELVES IN, AND... WELL, YOU KNOW!
Non-stop until we were dead tired!
Oh you...!
HUH, WOW!
That's good to hear.

THEN WE GOT TO TALKING ABOUT A LOT OF THINGS...

AND I THOUGHT, MAYBE I SHOULD LET YOU STAY ON THE ATTACK
WHILE I STAY BACK AND DEFEND.

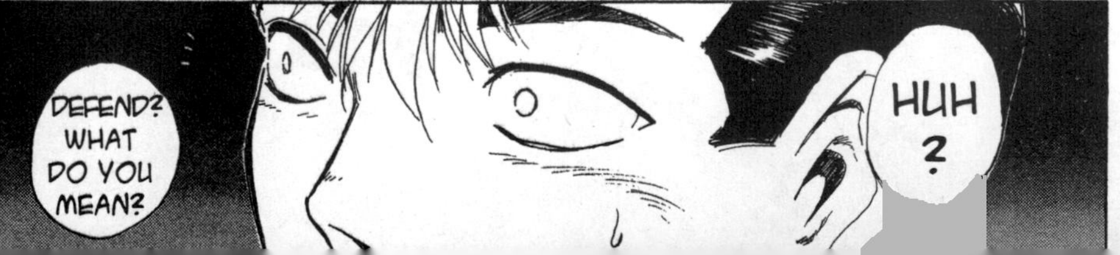
HUH?
DEFEND? WHAT DO YOU MEAN?

Have a kid
Egg club, chick club, chirp chirp!
and settle down.
たまごクラブ
EGG CLUB
カギーン
GOOOOONG
?!
I'M LEAVING IT TO YOU, EIKI-CHI.
OUR HAPPINESS IS GOING TO DEPEND ON YOU NOW.
PROTECT US WELL, OKAY?
Haha haha
Haha
Protect my nest!
HEY HO, SHONAN DEFENSE FORCE!
...

HAHAHA
TWITCH
YEAH, I'M JUST NO MATCH COMPARED TO DEMON EIKICHI!
...
HE'S A DEMON! REAL WARRIOR MEN ARE SOMETHING ELSE!
TWITCH
YOU'RE NOT TRYING TO HAND OFF
ALL YOUR DIRTY WORK TO ME, ARE YOU?
TWITCH

THAT'S NOT WHAT I'M SAYING AT ALL!
I JUST WANT BOTH OF US TO BE HAPPY.
I'D LIKE TO SEE YOU SETTLE DOWN SOME TIME SOON, TOO.
WE CAN PILE INTO A MINIVAN WITH BLISTER FENDERS AND TAKE OUR KIDS CAMPING.
Oni-Baku decals to top it off!
MY KID AND YOURS COULD GET TOGETHER AND MAKE THE ONI-BAKU JUNIOR ...
I BET IT'LL BE FUN.
RYUJI ...
YOU...

THOUGH ...
SHHT

it might be hard for a guy
to have a kid on his own.
PUFFF
?!

WELL, MAYBE THEY'LL FIGURE OUT HOW TO CLONE HUMANS IN ANOTHER FIVE YEARS!!
AHA-HAHA! THAT'S A GOOD ONE! NICE!
Cell division or something!
...
Y-YOU BAS-TARD...
GET-TING SO COCKY.
It's just my policy
not to have a girl.
IF I WANTED ONE...
I COULD HAVE ONE ANY TIME!
You oversexed freak!
Now, now...
DAM
YOU ASS...
KLATT
POP POP POP POP
SKRR
OH? THEN WHY DON'T YOU FORGET ABOUT THAT POLICY
AND TRY TO GET YOURSELF A GIRL?
Fwe he he
Puff
Ryuji...

POP POP POP POP
SKR
Kawasaki
KH
Benl

HM?
POP POP
HUH?

A KH-250?
A WOM-AN?

KLAK
KLAK
KLAK
JINGLE

ZAKK

HUH?

FWASH
CLIK
!!
...
SAYA ...
SHE'S SMOKING HOT ?!
A girl like that rides a KH-250?
SUP

KEEP ME COM-PANY TONIGHT.

WHERE'D YOU FIND HER ?!!
KLATT
Wha ?
WHAT ?! SHE KNOWS EIKICHI ?!

YOU CAN,
YES ?
HEH

UNDER-STAND NOW, RYUJI?
IF I ACTUALLY TRY, STUFF LIKE THIS IS NOTH-ING.

GRIN

WH-WHAT ?!

THAT'S IMPOSSIBLE. E-EIKICHI AND A HOT GIRL LIKE THAT? HAHA...
SKFF
HRN? I-IT'S NOT LIGHTING. YO, ANYONE GOT A...
SKFF

LIGHTER?

Here
?!
ポロ… PLOP
スゥーー SLIDE
...
バカッ BAKRAK
...
GSHHT
GSHHT
BRIGKT
...
...
WHY DON'T YOU DIE, RYUJI!
...
DIE!
...

C'MON, EIKICHI. LET'S GO.
I THOUGHT THAT YOU MIGHT BE FEELING RESTLESS
SO I CAME TO ASK.
Let's just go
and do it.

HUH?
D-DO IT??
COME, NOW.
THROB
I'M ALMOST ON my period AND
THROB
I'M ABOUT TO GET a nose-bleed.
THROB
My whole body's feeling hot.

?!
Plip
What ?!
H-HEY, EIKICHI! WAIT, WHERE ARE YOU...
Later!
EI-KICHI!
THIS IS THE DAY...
THUMP
THUMP
I GO ALL THE WAY.
STUP
THROB
YOU'LL GET ON,
WON'T YOU?
THROB
OH, I-I'LL GET ON, ALL RIGHT!
THUMP

THUMP
THUMP

# GTO The Early Years

## Chapter 207: GIVE ME BODY

NOTHING vibrates QUITE LIKE AN OLD TWO-STROKE ...

I JUST WANT TO SIT ON THIS SEAT FOREVER ...
Heh heh

POP POP
...
I'M SO excited ...
I'm going to be doing it
with you.

ARE YOU
REALLY FINE WITH ME?

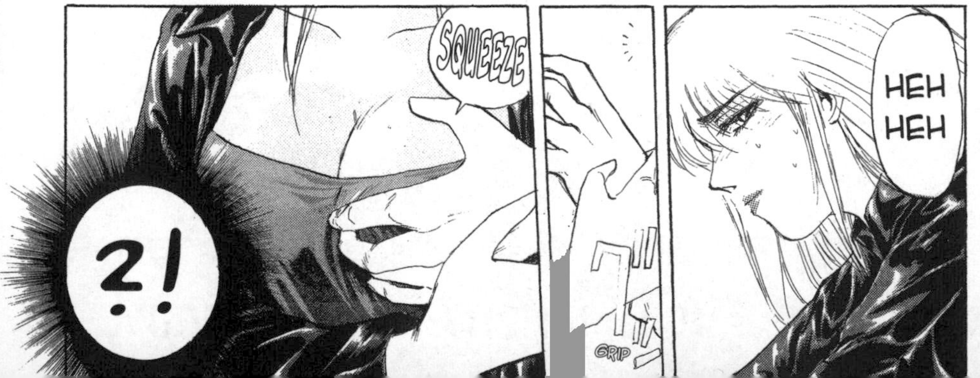
HEH HEH
GRIP
SQUEEZE
?!

HOLD ON TIGHT.
POP POP POP
SKRRR REE

THAT'S NO FAIR, EIKICHI!
Let me in on that!
POP POP POP
Ha ha!
Bye!
EIKICHI! WAIT, YOU ...!

EI-KICHI ...?

THIS TIME'S FOR REAL.
GRRRRRN

GWOOOMM
AT LAST I'LL BE DOING

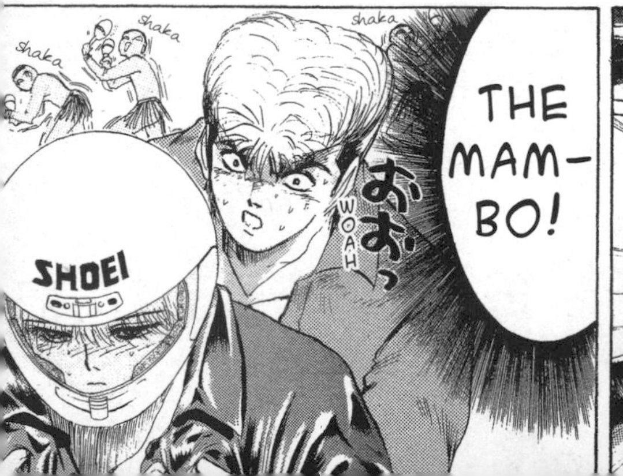
THE MAM-BO!
おおっ
WOAH
shaka
shaka
shaka
SHOEI

THAT RACE WAS RAD.
TO WIN IT ON THAT ZII...
IT MADE MY WHOLE BODY tingle.

Y-YUP
I'M GETTING ALL TINGLY DOWN-STAIRS, TOO.

THAT JOEY GUY WAS FAMOUS EVEN AMONG THE BLUE ROSE FOR BEING CRAZY
BUT YOU BEAT HIM WITHOUT EVEN USING YOUR FISTS.

I GUESS THE RUMORS WERE TRUE?
THAT YOU'RE ...
THE STRONG-EST AROUND IN KANA-GAWA.

I GUESS.
I'M GONNA DO IT
I'M GONNA DO IT
I'M GONNA DO IT
I'M GONNA DO IT
I'M GONNA DO IT
I'M GONNA DO IT
I'M GONNA DO IT
I'M GONNA DO IT
I'M GONNA DO IT
I'M GONNA DO IT
I'M GONNA DO IT
I'M GONNA DO IT
I'M GONNA DO IT

I BET ...

you'll make me do what you want
even if you had to spank me.
Y-YOU'D RUN THAT WAY?!!
From the first time?!
AAHHH ...
I CAN'T STAND IT ANY LONGER.
C'MON, LET'S GET STARTED.
HUH?
RIGHT HERE.
Come on, spank me.
Right here.
OUT IN THE OPEN ??
DOOM
MAYBE WE'LL START OFF IN A MORE PRIVATE PLACE?
DOESN'T MATTER.
IT GETS ME MORE heated up IF A CROWD IS WATCH-ING.
SKR

GWOM MM
GRRN NN
alway my make my drop my bad lov my
POP POP
Slam
They are like a mov on or on r the spy. a
?!

WAIT, HERE?
ARE YOU SERI-OUS?!
Let's get started ...
ALL RIGHT.

Things are going to get
real bloody, fast.

SHOCK
FIRST-TIME BLEEDING ?? WHAT A BONUS!!
FLAP
H-HEY, WAIT ...
I'M NOT READY YET...
KLIK KLIK

DOING IT WITH A VIRGIN THIS HOT WHO LIKES TO PLAY WITH HERSELF?
Here?!
Beckon
NAGISA'S NOT EVEN ON THE SAME LEVEL AS HER! I'M GOING TO BE LEAVING RYUJI WAY IN THE DUST!
I'll be a pro in no time!
STRIP
STRIP
GLOK
HUH ?

WHAT ARE YOU DOING, SAYA ?!
HYAAAGH!
BRAK
Gwa
What's with her ?!
!
GLAK
?!
Wha...
WHAT THE HELL ARE YOU DOING ?
ZSST
Loom
WHAT AM I DOING ?
ISN'T IT OBVIOUS ?

YOU SAID YOU'D DO IT WITH ME, DIDN'T YOU?
WE'RE CON-QUERING JAPAN.
GWOOOOSH
CON-QUER JAPAN ??
FINGERPRINT

SAYA MINAZUKI, HEAD OF THE YOKOSUKA FLAME DANCERS !!
IF YOU GOT A PROBLEM, JUST BRING IT ON!
S-Stop!
THUD
What the hell is wrong with you?
What's with this chick? She's nuts!
"DOING IT" USUALLY MEANS SEX!
In broad day-light...

NO ...
Don't forget this!
AFTER BEING STOKED LIKE THAT, I'LL BE LEFT WITH BLUE-BALLS ?
Hey!
Are you running away?

WHAT'S WRONG ?
Bam Brrm
AREN'T WE GONNA DO IT?

THUMP
WHAT'S THE SAD LOOK FOR?

DID YOU THINK THAT I MEANT SOME-THING ELSE
TWITCH
WHEN I SAID WE WERE GONNA DO IT?
...

WAIT A SEC ...

IDIOT
KRIK
WHO DO YOU THINK I AM ?
I HATE PICKING FIGHTS FOR NO GOOD REASON.

ISN'T THAT HOW
A REAL MAN OUGHT TO BE ?
OR AM I WRONG ?
...

YOU'RE RIGHT.

BEING WITH YOU,
I JUST FEEL SO PAIN-FULLY SMALL.
My prick feels pretty painful, too!
...
Dun-dun da-da daaan
Firing Wave Motion Gun in ten seconds!

EVER SINCE I TOOK OVER THE FLAME DANCERS
I'VE BEEN SO WORRIED ABOUT MAKING A NAME FOR MYSELF.

PHEW, I FEEL RELIEVED.
Somehow ...
Heh

YOU'RE PRETTY COOL, YOU KNOW THAT?
I HOPE I DON'T GET SERIOUS ABOUT YOU.
Not a good idea.

I STILL HAVE A CHANCE !!

SAYA...
WILL YOU
BE MY GIRL?
GO FOR IT!!
WHAT?
YOU KNOW...
ガシ
GRAB!!

I'VE BEEN SEARCHING SO LONG
FOR A WOMAN WHO COULD FOLLOW ME ALL THE WAY.
ONIZUKA...

REALLY?
I'M A BAD GIRL WHO PLAYS WITH HERSELF ALL DAY...

FINE BY ME...
THAT'S JUST WHAT I WANT!!
May I watch?

I CAN'T LET
ONIZUKA
THIS CHANCE GET AWAY!

THUMP
THUMP
THUMP
I'M GONNA DO IT
TODAY, I'LL...!
Don't go
easy on me.

ぎゃはははは
GYAHAHAHA
Gya ha ha ha!
Are you stupid or something?!
What an idiot!
I hope you die!!
Fingerprint
CLICK
MD
WHAT'RE YOU TRYING TO LOOK COOL FOR, SQUID MAN?
Ah!! Shinomi?! W-Why?
IF SHE WENT OUT WITH A LAME-ASS LIKE YOU, HER LIFE WOULD BE OVER ON THE SPOT!
SH-SH-SHINOMI? YOU WERE LISTENING?!
YEP! AND I GOT IT ALL RECORDED ON MD, TOO!
It's digital!
THE HELL ARE YOU?

I'VE BEEN TAKING CARE OF THIS IDIOT SINCE HE WAS IN JUNIOR HIGH.
You brat!
YOU WERE PRETTY CLOSE TO THE LEDGE.
HE MIGHT FOOL YOU WITH HIS BIG TALK, BUT HE'S REALLY JUST A PRICK.
Tiny, too.
HEY, WATCH IT!
WELL, NOW THAT I'M HERE, YOU'RE SAFE.
...
I'LL TELL YOU ALL ABOUT HOW HE REALLY IS.
Just go away!
Keep your big nose out of this, hag.
HAH?
Hag?
SWOOP
SHATTER
ICK?

Worry about yourself first...
stinky bitch.

COME ON, ONIZUKA, LET'S GO.
Let's get to a hotel.
H-HEY! WHAT HAVE YOU DONE?
Shinomi! Are you okay?

WHO ARE YOU GOING TO CHOOSE, ME OR HER?
I'll let you do anything you want with me.

Well, if you put it that way...
Then leave her.
Well, uh, I mean...

HEY, GIRL?

THUD
?!

You do some pretty stupid things, don't you?!
LICK
Fine then ... bring it on!

DO YOU KNOW WHO I AM, YOU BITCH?
GRIT

H-HEY! WHAT ARE YOU TWO GETTING SO WORKED UP—

BAM
!!

I'll leave you covered in your own blood!
BWAM
Bring it!!
WAAAAAA AAAGH!!
SHHK
THUD
BEAUTIES LIKE YOU TWO, FIGHTING IN BROAD DAYLIGHT?
HUH?
?!

It's not good
for women to fight.
Grip
Dig
N-NAKAJO?!
Good timing!
C'MON, TALK TO ME.
I'LL LISTEN.

THUD
I, KUNITO NAKAJO FROM ENO COM—
Gahh ?
THUD
GSSHT
GSHT
RYAAAAGH!
BKKT
BRGT
You ugly bitch !!! ...
A-ARE YOU OKAY, NAKAJO ?!!
...?!
Haah?! You're the one who needs a facelift!!

GYAHAHAHAHA
HAHAHA
HEHEHE
Pfff ff
GTO The Early Years
Chapter 208:
ON NIGHTS YOU FALL IN LOVE

SO, WHAT? BY "DO IT" SHE MEANT ZANY SHIT LIKE CONQUER JAPAN?!
GYAHAHAHA! "REAL MEN" ARE A BREED APART!
...
I THOUGHT IT WAS WEIRD! A CHICK LIKE THAT PICKING YOU OUT...
WHY DON'T YOU STAY THE BOSS OF SHONAN FOR THE REST OF YOUR LIFE?
Gyahahaha!
You can't beat this!
SHAKE
SHAKE
Y-YOU GUYS...
YOU'RE JUST GOING TO LAUGH IT UP
WHEN YOUR FRIEND'S IN THE PITS??
TWITCH
TWITCH
OH, DON'T GET SO UPSET, EIKICHI.

ALL I'M TRYING TO SAY IS THAT GIRLS AREN'T ALL THERE IS TO LIFE.
WHY NOT SEE THIS AS A CALL TO REBOUND WITH A **guy**?
TWITCH
I BET KATSUYUKI WILL BE HARD TO GIVE UP!!
Daahaha!
I bet this guy's got a tight ass!
H-HEY! KNOCK IT OFF...
PLOP

GONG
BBT
Y-YOU BASTARD... I'M BLEEDING NOW. SEE?!
Uh
YOU WANT YOUR BRAINS TO COME OUT NEXT?
Bring it!
HEY, DON'T GET SO UPSET OVER SOMETHING LIKE THIS.
JUST GIVE IT UP! YOU'VE JUST NEVER HAD ANY LUCK WITH WOMEN.
ARE YOU TRYING TO TELL ME THAT YOU DO?
EVEN THOUGH YOU CRIED AFTER GETTING DUMPED ONCE?
TWITCH
HUH?
NO, I THINK RYUJI'S JUST FINE.
What do you mean by that?
SEE, IN THIS NAME HOROSCOPE BOOK...
WHA?
THE CHARACTERS FOR "RYUJI DANMA" ARE WRITTEN IN 41 strokes, RIGHT?
I think...
IT SAYS HERE, "YOU WILL GAIN FAME AND FORTUNE, AND LIVE A HAPPY LIFE."
WHAT?!
THAT'S RIDICULOUS! L-LET ME SEE THAT!
SNATCH
"PEOPLE WITH 41-STROKE NAMES ARE UPRIGHT AND HATE WRONGDOING."
"THEY ARE SOCIABLE AND GENTLE, BUT BRAVE."
Gloom

Hahahaha
YEAH, MAKES SENSE! I DID THINK AS MUCH!
"Sociable and gentle, but brave," huh? Makes sense that I'm good with the ladies...
Me next.
DON'T BE STUPID!!
W-WELL, MY NAME ...
LET'S SEE HERE, 36 strokes ...
FLIP
FLIP
FLIP

A life of chivalry full of ups and downs.
The more you try, the deeper you will be dragged into a quagmire. A life of quick rises and steep falls.

GYAHA HAHA! A life of chivalry! THIS THING'S SPOT ON!
Hee hee hee hee
I THINK YOUR LIFE IS OVER, MAN! GYAA HAHA!
Uh, you... That's Eikichi... So cool...
Bwa ha ha
HM-PH...
YOU GUYS DON'T UNDERSTAND ANYTHING.
Pop
JUST THINK ABOUT IT.
THE FACT IS THAT TWO GIRLS GOT IN A FIGHT OVER ME.
Hee hee hee

IN OTHER WORDS, THEY'RE BOTH HOT FOR ME, RIGHT?
DON'T YOU SEE? I'VE GOT TWO GIRLS IN LOVE WITH ME.
Two girls. Two!
?!
IF I WANTED, THEY'D GLADLY OPEN UP THEIR...
HM?
Who's going to
open what up?

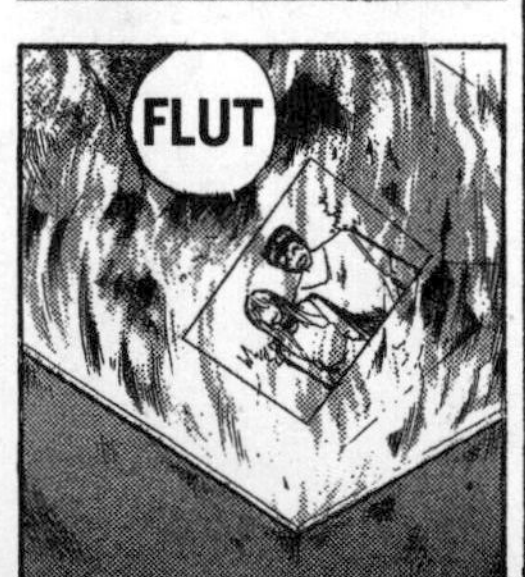


## 41

**Luck that will bring you success, wealth, and fame. A clean, straight-forward person.**

Those with 41 strokes are straightforward and hate injustice. They have calm and gentle personalities, and are also brave and knowledgeable. As a result, they are able to gain fame and fortune. However, in modern society, where one needs to defeat others in order to come out ahead, their tolerant personalities are likely to cause them to suffer.

SNAP
KRAKLE
...
HEH
FLUT
GOOD-BYE...
AYUMI MURA-KOSHI...
flap
HM? WAIT A SECOND ...
WHAT ABOUT THE PICTURE WE TOOK WHEN WE FIRST MET IN OKINAWA?
WHAT ARE YOU BURN-ING?
Ah!
NO-THING AT ALL!
Hahaha!
THUD
POP
CRACKLE
CRACKLE
BLAZE

GAH, I'M SO HUN-GRY!
Hahaha...
HEY, LET'S HURRY UP AND EAT!
...

ALL RIGHT, I'LL MAKE A FEAST TONIGHT ♡
HUH?
MY NAGISA SPECIAL PORK SUKIYAKI♡
We're on a budget.
HUH? P-PORK??
Don't get greedy!
But!

KINDERGARTEN
AHA HA!
TEE HEE!

BYE, MS. MURA-KOSHI!
Thanks!
BYE!
MS. MURA-KOSHI, YOU HAVE A GUEST!
OKAY!

YO
FUMI-YA...
SO, HOW'S IT GOIN'?
WELL, YOU KNOW THE BIG OUTDOOR PARTY IS COMING UP. I'M EX-HAUSTED!
I SEE.
YOU'RE DONE FOR THE DAY, RIGHT?
I'LL TAKE YOU HOME.
Who's Ayumi talking to?
He's cute!
Thanks
HEY, WHO'S THAT BOY?
NOT YOUR BOY TOY, IS HE?
He's kinda handsome
YUP, BOY TOY!
POM
N-NO! FUMI-YA!
No way?! Seri-ously??!

THAT'S NOT
HOW IT IS WITH US.
...

HEY, AYUMI.
DID SOME-THING HAPPEN?

HUH?
YOU KNOW, YOU MET RYUJI THE OTHER DAY.
SOME-THING THEN?
...
NO-THING AT ALL.
THERE'S NOTHING BETWEEN ME
AND RYUJI NOW.
...
AH ...

SO THAT MEANS I'M FREE
TO GO AFTER YOU ?

HUH? WHAT ?!
I can't hear...
HAHA... NOTHING.

HOLD ON, I'M GONNA FLOOR IT!
Ah, wait !
Sto ...
Aa-ah!
Ahh!
Ha ha

DON'T BE A DARE-DEVIL !
KLAK
HAHA! I SAID THAT YOU'D BE FINE. I'M A GENIUS ON A BIKE, YOU KNOW ?
JUST MY POINT ...

JUST LET ME CHANGE REAL FAST.
KLAK

CLUNK

PHEW, IT'S COLD!

GREE
AYUMI, CAN YOU MAKE ME SOMETHING WARM TO EAT?

OH, YOU'RE JUST AS SHAMELESS AS ALWAYS!
OOH, I'M HUNGRY !
He he

HUH ?

...

UH-OH!
I FORGOT TO GIVE HIM THIS ONE.

I THOUGHT I'D GIVEN HIM ALL OF THEM.

CHANGE OF PLANS! I'LL MAKE DINNER, AFTER ALL!
PULL
I MAKE A PRETTY MEAN STEW!
FUMIYA
COME ON, SIT DOWN.
H-HEY—!
Can you really cook?
I'm a genius at cooking!
Are you sure?
Chatter Chatter
GYA HAHA! SAEJIMA,
YOUR PALM SAYS YOU'VE GOT BAD LUCK WITH GIRLS!
Woah, it's true!
WHAT'RE YOU BLABBERING ON ABOUT, IDIOTS?!
JUST STOP MESSING AROUND AND HELP ME WITH THIS MAINTENANCE.
Ha ha
HEY!
FWOM
FWOM
SKRR
...
DWOOM
DWOOM

Shit!
Twitch
Y-YOU ...!
FUMIYA!
THE HELL ARE YOU SHOWING YOUR FACE AROUND HERE FOR?!
HAH?
MOVE
I SAID, MOVE.

THIS DOESN'T CONCERN YOU, **pencil nose.**
Bcht

WHAT THE HELL DID YOU SAY?! I'LL KILL YOU!!
H-HEY, SAEJIMA! C'MON, LET'S GO HOME!
I'LL KILL YOUUU!
OKAY, NOW ...
WHAT IS IT, FUMI-YA?
...
Shin-doji, you...!
Sae-jima...

...
I'M NEVER GOING TO LOSE
TO YOU, OR TO MY BRO-THER!
I'VE... MADE UP MY MIND.

I'LL GET HER TO SAY

WHAAAA?
What're you...
I'M THE BEST MAN SHE'S EVER MET!
HEY, FUMIYA! WHAT DO YOU MEAN BY THAT?!
I'm not gonna lose to you!
Huuh?
I'm not!
RUSTLE
H- HEY! SAE-JIMA!!
SHUSH
RUSTLE

GLEAM
Today's the day
I pencil-nose him back!!

HOLD ON, SAEJIMA!!
What do you mean?
Hahaha!
SHUT UP!
I'LL NEVER FORGET THAT PAIN...
IF YOU THINK SNAKES ARE TENACIOUS...
RUSTLE
SHIFT

JERK
WAIT TILL YOU GET THIS!
Now's my chance to pencil-nose him!!

GKKT
YHUP...
ZBBT
Yeaaaaaaaaaagh!!!...
SAEJI-MAAAA?!
He got pencil-nosed!!
HM? I THINK I STEPPED ON SOME-THING.
Shake
HEY, WHAT'S WRONG? WHY DO YOU HAVE PENCILS STUCK IN YOUR NOSE?
You want to apolo-gize?
P-P-P-Pencils in my nose?!!
?
CALL AN AMBU-LANCE!

GTO The Early Years
Chapter 209:
TO MY SON...

FWAP
WOW, YOU'RE DOING LAUNDRY. ONLY 17 AND ALREADY A FULL-FLEDGED HOUSEWIFE!
I couldn't myself ...
WHAT? THAT'S NOT TRUE!
A HOUSEWIFE? THAT'S JUST...
I'M STILL NOT ...
HM ?
WHAT'S WRONG? WORRIED ABOUT SOMETHING?
HUH? W-WELL...
ACTUALLY, I'M A LITTLE LATE THIS MONTH, IF YOU KNOW WHAT I MEAN...
WHAT ?

FIRST YOU'RE A HOUSEWIFE, NOW YOU'RE GOING TO BE A MOM?
Trying to pass it off as nothing!
Oh, don't jump to conclusions!
I DON'T KNOW FOR SURE YET.
YOU SHOULD GET IT CHECKED OUT.
AT A HOSPITAL, WHILE IT'S STILL EARLY.
IT'S A LIFETIME ISSUE.
...
... YEAH.
YOU'RE RIGHT.
A LIFETIME
ISSUE ...

BUT MAN, WHAT A FIASCO!
YOU GETTING PENCIL-NOSED AGAIN!
...
WHAT A SURPRISE!
FOR IT TO BE A JOKE, YOU WERE BLEEDING TOO MUCH!
I laughed though.
BUT WHY DID THAT HAPPEN ANYWAY?
YOU DIDN'T END UP STABBING YOUR OWN NOSE WHILE YOU WERE TRYING TO GET FUMIYA, DID YOU? THAT'D JUST BE WAY TOO GREAT!
TWITCH
...

...
YEP, EXACTLY.
I WAS TRYING TO PENCIL-NOSE HIM BUT STABBED MY OWN NOSE INSTEAD.
HEH, I GUESS IT'S FUNNY...
YOU GUYS CAN LAUGH...
I DON'T MIND. GO AHEAD, IF YOU WANT TO.

GYAAAHAHA
HEE HEE HEE
Gyaa-haha! It really is true!
It really was a "self-pencil-nose"!
Heee-hehee
WHA?

I KNEW YOU WERE INTO THAT STUFF
...
BUT I NEVER THOUGHT YOU'D DO IT TO YOURSELF!!
M-My sides...!
Gyaahahaha
YOU'RE REALLY ON TO SOMETHING HERE, BEING SO BIG OF AN IDIOT!! AHAHAHA!
Y-YOU BASTARD...
I'll kill you.
TWITCH
Heee-hehehe
THUMP
Wheez wheez

OH, HERE YOU ARE!
KLAK
WHAT IS IT, EIKICHI? ARE YOU HERE TO LAUGH AT ME TOO?
HUH?
WHAT ARE YOU TALKING ABOUT? I'M JUST HERE TO VISIT YOU.
ARE YOU OKAY, SAE-JIMA?
I THOUGHT YOU MIGHT BE FEELING DOWN SINCE YOU GOT HURT.
SO, I BROUGHT YOU SOME FLOWERS.
HERE

PLEASE, ACCEPT THESE
pencil roses.
I'LL NEVER FORGIVE YOU... LAUGHING AT SOMEONE WHO'S SUFFERING SO MUCH.
I'LL MAKE YOU ALL SUFFER, TOO!!
WHAT DO YOU GUYS THINK ??
SPIN
Gyaaahaha! pencil roses! That's so dumb!!
SHAKE SHAKE
...
Heeehehehehe
C'MON, GIMME YOUR NOSES !!
Kyaaahahaha
Oh, sir!
WOAH! DON'T PUSH YOURSELF, YOU'RE GOING TO GET ANOTHER NOSE-BLEED!
COME BACK HERE, YOU!
Wheez wheez
MAN, THAT GUY IS GREAT TO MAKE FUN OF.
HEY! YOU TRYING TO RUN?!
P-Please! Your wounds will reopen!
SHING
...
IT'S THE CON-TRAST WITH THAT SCARY FACE OF HIS !
You're horrible, Ryuji.

Yeah?
LET'S COME POKE FUN AT HIM AGAIN.
YEAH, WE'LL BRING SOME FRESH PENCILS!
Gya-hahaha-ha!
HM?
OH!
HM? NAGISA?
what're you doing here?
Hahaha
HUH? OH, I'M ...
Haha
UH-OH.
WHAT'S WRONG? ARE YOU FEELING A LITTLE ...
HM?
Obstetrics and Gynecology
HM?
...
WHAT'S WRONG, RYU...

SILENCE
しーーん
Obstetrics and Gynecology
...
...
HA HA
...
Y-YOU'RE GETTING IT WRONG, RYUJI! I'M JUST A LITTLE LATE THIS MONTH...
I JUST CAME BECAUSE I WAS A LITTLE WORRIED...
Con-grats, Ryuji!
TOOT
POP
Congratulations! Junior's on the way!
Ha ha ha
Ha ha ha
Woo!
Clap clap
HUH?

WELL, YOU'VE DONE IT! YOU'RE GONNA BE A dad!
Are you serious? Wha?!
Aw jeez...
Huh?
Huh?
Huh?
Huh?
SO FAST, TOO. IT HASN'T EVEN BEEN A WEEK SINCE YOU DECLARED YOU WERE SETTLING DOWN.
Look at you!
N-NO, YOU SEE, I'M SAYING...
I'm just late this month!
WOW, A DAD WHILE STILL IN HIGH SCHOOL...
Maybe we should start calling you the Stallion of Tsujido!

IF YOU'RE GONNA HAVE A KID, IT'S GOT TO BE A BOY.
YOU CAN GIVE HIM SPECIAL LESSONS FROM A YOUNG AGE SO HE CAN AIM TO CONQUER ALL JAPAN!
NO WAY, A GIRL WOULD BE WAY BETTER.
WAIT, I'M ONLY ...
AIDS
Hahahaha
HAVE A CUTE DAUGHTER, THRUST HER INTO SHOW BIZ AND GET RICH!
How's being a stage father sound? Haha!
Hmm ...
ooh!
Guys around the country will be getting off to your daughter! Isn't that awesome?!
No, a boy is really way better...
IT'S FINE.
DON'T YOU WORRY ABOUT A THING.
PAT
LEAVE IT TO ME.
TO Daddy Ryuji.
ALL RIGHT, STARTING TODAY, I'M GONNA HUNKER DOWN AND WORK MY ASS OFF!
I mean, I'm gonna be a dad! Mmmm!
I'm telling you, no!
BONK
BONK
BONK
OKAY, WE'RE ALL GOING OUT FOR A DRINK, MY TREAT!
Hahaha
Whoooo!
TH-THIS IS BAD ...
THEY HAVE ME ALL WRONG ...
I-I'M ONLY THREE DAYS LATE RIGHT NOW!!

再診受付
STARE

WHAT'S WRONG, LITTLE GUY?
YOU GET SEPA-RATED FROM YOUR MOTHER?
Why don't you talk to Daddy Ryuji?

HYUP
HM? I FEEL LIKE I'VE SEEN THIS KID BEFORE...

HEEEY! IF IT ISN'T RYUJI!

MISTER SANO?!
From the Midnight Angels?
Wait, Sano? You mean?
Hahaha!
WOW!
YOU REALLY SURPRISED ME! I MEAN, JUST LOOK AT THOSE OUTDOORSY CLOTHES!
Hey, it's what's in right now!

WHAT HAPPENED, RYUJI? I WOULDN'T EXPECT TO SEE YOU IN A HOSPITAL.
DID SOME-THING HAP— HM?

HUH?

SO THAT'S WHAT IT IS! YOU MIGHT BE A DAD PRETTY SOON! AHAHA!
NOOOOO!
Yep, that's it.

WELL, SINCE I'M YOUR SENIOR WHEN IT COMES TO HAVING A KID...
Oh!
HOW ABOUT YOU COME OVER TO MY HOUSE RIGHT NOW?
I'LL TREAT YOU TO A DRINK OR SOMETHING.
Whoooo!
Pat
WHAT? SERIOUSLY?
ALL RIGHT, LET'S GO!
LISTEN, I'M TRYING TO TELL YOU ...
Aahahahahaha!
This is great news!
Aha ha
Ha ha
MAN, TO THINK THAT THE COCKY LITTLE BRAT IS GOING TO BE A DAD!
ははははは
HAHAHAHA
...
AND YOU? YOU'VE TOTALLY SETTLED DOWN!
THIS IS BAD.
AT THIS RATE, IT'LL JUST SNOWBALL... WHAT TO DO?
MISTER SANO REALLY USED TO BE SOMETHING!
HEY NOW, LET'S NOT TALK ABOUT THE PAST.
It's embarrassing!
HE USED TO BE CALLED THE "GOD OF WAR" AND HAD EYES LIKE THIIIS!
Real scary!
H-Hey! Hahaha...
WOW! R-REALLY?
I can't see that at all.

TA-DAAAA
SEE, HERE'S AN OLD PIC OF HIM.
Here's me, and Eikichi's by my side.
WHICH ONE IS MISTER SANO?
THIS ONE HERE...
HUH?
TH-THIS GUY???
H-He looks like a demon!
Another great day to wear your baggy pants and fix your pompadour
Yay
AW JEEZ...
How embarrassing! Hahaha...
YEP, I SURE WAS YOUNG BACK THEN!
WHAT ARE YOU SAYING? YOU'RE STILL ONLY 18!
E-EIGHTEEN?!
With that moustache?
SO YOU GOT MARRIED...
WHEN I WAS 15.
It wasn't official until recently, though.
Dad
FIFTEEN?!
Tenth grade?
YEP!
I'M HOME!
OH, WELCOME BACK!
S-SO THEN...
YOUR WIFE...
WELCOME!
I'm Chinami, seventeen years old!
I bought some drinks!
?!

OH, HERE SHE IS! THE SHONAN MANDALA LADIES' SHOCK TROOPER!
You were famous for hating men back then!
Chinami in the past
OH, DON'T BRING UP OLD STORIES LIKE THAT!
I feel like these two looked older back then...
...
JUN AND I HAVE MOVED PAST THOSE DAYS!
NOW I'M JUST YOUR AVERAGE HOUSE-WIFE.
I MAKE CLOTHES FOR MY BOY ON A SEWING MACHINE!
Come on try it on!
RUSTLE
HERE, COME ON!
ISN'T IT CUTE?
Check out all the letterings!
AWWW
Yaay!
WOAH, A BIKER'S ROBE!
TA-DAAAAA
I WAS THINKING OF TAKING HIM LIKE THIS TO OUR NEXT OLD BOYS' MEETING!
Man, that's great!
THAT'S AWE-SOME!
I envy you! What a great couple!
...
N-NO WAY...
THE LAST THING I WANT
IS TO BECOME A "FORMER YANQUI" MOM...
When you have your own kid, let's go camping together!
sounds great
ANYWAY, YOU CHOOSE A NAME YET, RYUJI?
It's tough! Gotta mind the number of strokes and all.
WELL, WE HAVEN'T GOTTEN TO THAT YET...
U-UM—
I'D LIKE A CUTE NAME...
Like "Kirin"
WELL, A MAN'S GOT TO HAVE A TOUGH NAME.
Like "Goki"!
Or "Bunta"!
Gokuji is good too!
NOOOO!

NO, NOT THIS!
If it's a girl, how about "Onihime"!
No way, it'll be "Bakudanko"!
Or "Akuma"!
I HAVE MY OWN DREAM!
I WANT MY CHILD TO HAVE A REGULAR GIRLISH NAME
Hahaha
AND TO WEAR CUTE CLOTHES, WHILE WE PICNIC...
Open wide!
NO ASSEMBLIES OR BIKER ROBES...
I JUST WANT TO BE A NORMAL WIFE!

WELL, I DON'T REALLY CARE IF IT'S A BOY OR A GIRL
AS LONG AS SHE HAS A HEALTHY BABY
THAT I CAN RAISE WITH HER.
Hey, are you bragging about your wife?
Well, ha ha ha!
...

STUPID ME...
HE'S SUCH A FIND!
But you're showing off too, Sano!
Let me do a little bragging too!
NORMALLY, WHEN A GIRL MY AGE GETS PREGNANT, THE GUY TURNS BLUE TO DENY IT'S HIS OR ASKS THAT SHE GET RID OF IT.
I'VE HEARD THAT KIND OF STORY PLENTY OF TIMES.
BUT YOU, YOU LOOK SO HAPPY ABOUT IT.

I LOVE YOU, RYUJI...
WITH YOU, I'M READY FOR ANY FUTURE.
I'M SURE OF IT...
WELL... ONCE YOU HAVE A KID, DRIVING AROUND BECOMES TOUGH!
FOR A MAN, FINDING A HOUSE IS SECONDARY. FIRST, FIGURE OUT YOUR CAR!
That's right!
I MEAN, I DROPPED 10 MIL INTO MODIFYING THE HECK OUT OF MINE!
Wanna see?
TEN MIL ?!
Say what?!
MY CAR'S PRETTY AMAZING!
I mean it's got gull-wings!
SEE, OVER THERE!

Mmff, that hurts, I...oh...
NGGGGT
PEOOOOOO
SNNNNN

ONCE I SAW RYUJI'S FACE, I JUST...
COULDN'T TELL HIM I'M ONLY THREE DAYS LATE.
I MEAN, HE JUST LOOKS SO HAPPY.
... AND I'M
HAPPY, TOO...
SNORE
ZZZZZZ

HEY, NAGISA ...
ARE YOU REALLY OKAY WITH IT?

IF YOU REALLY ARE PREG-NANT...
...
COULD YOU KEEP LIVING LIKE THIS?

YOU'RE STILL A RUNAWAY. YOU CAN'T EXPECT TO MAKE IT IN THIS CITY.
AT SEVENTEEN AND A BABY IN YOUR ARMS, COULD YOU
DITCH YOUR PARENTS ...
LEAVE SHO-NAN ...

AND BE ALL RIGHT?
I KNOW...
I KNOW
I'M BEING RASH.
I KNOW, BUT...
IN THE END...
I JUST LOVE
RYUJI
...

DO YOU THINK I'M LOOKING AT THIS WRONG?
I WONDER IF I'M GOING TO REGRET THIS LATER?
WHAT DO YOU THINK, SHINOMI?
ガシ GRAB
WHO CARES IF YOU'LL REGRET IT.
JUST AS LONG AS
IT'S YOUR OWN CHO-ICE.

HUH ...?

HA HA HA, DON'T TELL ME ...
YOU'RE NOT GOING TO PULL SOME OLD-TIMEY GAG ON ME AND SAY "I JUST HAD IT," ARE YOU?
...

HM?
WHAT'S WRONG, NAGISA?

...

D-DID YOU REALLY JUST HAVE IT?!
GRAB
...
Nod
That's like something out of a comic!

WH ...
WHAT SHOULD I DO?

命名 流弥
弾間
THE NAME: RYUYA DANMA
BROTHER
WHAT SHOULD YOU DO?
...
THAT'S A GOOD QUES-TION...
Just look at how psyched they are.
Mfff Ryuya

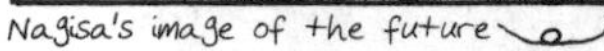
Nagisa's image of the future

# Chapter 210: SAND SHIP

Ryuji's image of the future

WHA-AAT?! YOU STILL HAVEN'T TOLD HIM??!
YEAH ...

"YEAH"? WHY HAVEN'T YOU YET? TELL HIM YOU AREN'T PREGNANT!
ガッ GRAB
SO DOES HE STILL THINK HE'S GOING TO BE A DADDY?!
YUP.
I KEEP MEANING TO TELL HIM...
BUT WHEN I SEE HIM LIKE THAT, I JUST CAN'T.
LIKE THAT?
HEY, NAGISA! I'M DONE!
I'M CALLING IT THE CHICK BUS!
じゃーーーん TA=DAAA
Haaahahaha
流弥くん
CONGRATULATIONS! WELCOME RYUYA!
Chickdes-Benz
HOW DO YOU LIKE IT? NOW WE'RE READY FOR HIM TO BE BORN AT ANY TIME!
Just call me Bob the Builder!
HEY, RYUJI. YOU SHOULD CUT OUT THE —
Man I did such a good job!
RIGHT?
...

PAT
WHAT ARE YOU SAYING, SHINOMI?
YOU'LL SEE WHEN YOU HAVE YOUR OWN KID!
WANT ONE NOW?
I CAN ASK EIKICHI FOR YOU!
If you have one now, they'll be in the same class year!
NO NEED FOR THAT!!
HEY, NAGISA!!
Do something about that hyper dad!
B-BUT...
OH NO!
I FORGOT TO BUY SOMETHING.
Ha haha
Jeez... Am I too wrapped up in this?
A pre-natal care book!
I'M GOING TO GO SHOPPING FOR A BIT.
HUH? WHAT ARE YOU GOING TO GET?
All right, I'm off!
Ha ha ha ha ha
Just wait, Ryuya!
H-Hey!
Ryu-ji!!
HMM... I SEE.
SO BABIES CAN HEAR VOICES WHILE STILL IN THE WOMB... HMMM...
Hey, you take a look at this too!
When you play music to it, it doesn't have to be classical.
Then I better teach him how to pick a fight.
...

I JUST CAN'T TELL HIM...

What?! You were lying?!!
You better have a good excuse!!
GRRT
TWITCH

Furniture Corner
Huh?
Hmm... What else?
IF I TELL HIM NOW...

UH, I WASN'T LYING...
I WAS REALLY ONLY FOUR DAYS LATE...
Whaat?

You bitch!! Do you enjoy lying to me?!!
SMAAASH
Daddy, stop!
Nooo! Honey, please stop!
IS THAT HOW HE'LL BE?

Not by a long shot, Nagisa...

Things are going to get awful at this rate!
OH, WHAT SHOULD I DO?

HEEY!

Furniture Corner
SHOVE
HOW DO YOU LIKE THIS FOR A STUDY DESK?
HAHAHAHA
RYUJI-!!

Furniture Corner
NO!! WE DON'T NEED ANYTHING LIKE THAT!
REALLY? YOU CAN ADJUST THE HEIGHT WITH THIS CRANK.
See?
TURN, TURN

THEN, LET ME JUST BUY THIS PRENATAL CONVERSATION SET...
Haha ha
Excuse me, I'll take this-
NOOOO!

I'M NOT PREGNANT.
I WAS MISTAKEN.

HUH?

THERE'S NO...

BABY.

WHAT?!
JERK
Ahh! Don't hit me!!

I'M SORRY...
I DID SOMETHING THAT MADE YOU MISUNDERSTAND.

...

...
I SEE ...

SO THERE WAS NO BABY!
...
HAH, I SEE ...

I'M SORRY.

YEAH ...
IT REALLY IS TOO SOON.

IF WE SUD-DENLY HAD A KID
YOU'D BE IN A FIX.

I OUGHT TO SPEAK TO YOUR FOLKS.

WHAT?

N-NO! I'M...
BE-FORE ANY-THING ...

IF THEY GIVE US THEIR BLESSING, WE WON'T HAVE TO WORRY
WHEN WE DO MAKE A BABY!

RYU-JI?

PAT

LET'S TRY AGAIN.
TIME IS ON OUR SIDE!

GRAB

YEAH ...

All right, how about some food?
Some-thing that'll give me a bunch of stam-ina!
Oh you...
OPEN

RYUJI!

THUD
HAH
HAH
HAH
THUD
HAH

HMM? WHAT'S WRONG, MAKOTO?
A-A BUNCH OF COPS AND CITY STAFF SHOWED UP

AND ARE SWARMING AROUND YOUR BUS!
WHAT?!

GSHT
STAMP

ガァァ
GRRRRRMMMMMM
RAT-
TLE

?!
BRKT
Ksht
GGGT
RATTLE
WHA...
ALL RIGHT!
GGGGT
WHAT THE HELL ARE YOU DOING?!
WHAT ARE YOU DOING TO MY HOME? HEY!!
ROAR
HEY?!!

STOOOP!
DASH

BASTARD!!
HEY, YOU!
KRAK

CLAMP

WHAT ARE YOU DOING TO RYUJI?
LET HIM GO!
HEY YOU!

DAD?!
...

WAS THIS YOU, DAD? YOU CALLED THE POLICE, DIDN'T YOU?!
WHY? WHY WOULD YOU DO THIS...
...
...

TO BRING YOU BACK HOME, NAGISA.
DON'T YOU DARE DO THIS FOR MY SAKE!

I'M NOT GOING HOME! I'M GOING TO BE WITH RYUJI!!

I'LL NEVER FORGIVE YOU FOR DOING THIS...
NA-GI-SA!

SMACK

IT'S TIME TO SNAP OUT OF THIS!

...

UAAA-AGH! LET ME GO!
I SAID LET ME GOOO!

Let go, bastards!!

YAAAAA
ARGH!!

WE WERE POWER-LESS.
SKREE
!
WE THOUGHT WE WERE INVINCIBLE, BUT...
IN THE END, ALL WE COULD DO
WAS KNEEL ...
MERELY LIE PRONE.

AND JUST LIKE THAT, THE CASTLE OF OUR DREAMS

FELL WITHOUT A FIGHT —

HEY, EIKICHI!
HAHA... LOOK, ISN'T IT AWE-SOME?

FROM TODAY ON

THIS WILL BE OUR CASTLE.

I GUESS IT'S GONE.
OUR CAS-TLE...
RYUJI GOT HAULED OFF AND IS STILL WITH THE COPS.
WHAT ABOUT NAGISA?
LOOKS LIKE THEY ENDED UP TAKING HER BACK HOME.
I SEE...
THERE WAS SO MUCH IN STORE
FOR THOSE TWO.
ANYTIME WE TRY TO DO SOMETHING ON OUR OWN
IT'S ADULTS WHO GET IN OUR WAY.

...
YEAH

WHY CAN'T THEY JUST LEAVE US ALONE ?
album

GTO
The Early Years
Chapter 211: RUN, BABY!!

GOT IT?
THAT PARK IS STATE-OWNED.
JUST BECAUSE THERE'S A BUS SITTING THERE DOESN'T MEAN YOU CAN LIVE IN IT.
THIS FALLS UNDER WRONGFUL POSSESSION OF PUBLIC PROPERTY IN THE PENAL CODE... IT'S A CRIME.
ON TOP OF THAT, YOU BROUGHT A RUNAWAY GIRL WITH YOU.
...
JUST HOW MANY TIMES ARE WE GOING TO HAVE TO BRING YOU IN HERE,
HUH?
WELL, I'LL LET YOU GO FOR TODAY, SINCE YOUR DAD AND I ARE OLD FRIENDS.
Y'HEAR ME? YOU NEED TO TRY AND LEARN FROM YOUR FATHER...
THEY JUST FINISHED TAKING A STATEMENT FROM HER, SO SHE'S ABOUT TO LEAVE.
LOOKS LIKE SHE WAS GOING TO SOME FANCY GIRLS' SCHOOL, HUH?
PUNKS LIKE YOU DON'T LIVE IN THE SAME WORLD.
...
NAGISA...
WHAT HAP-PENED TO HER?
SIR! PLEASE WAIT, HE'S STILL BEING QUES-TIONED!
STEP
STEP

BAM

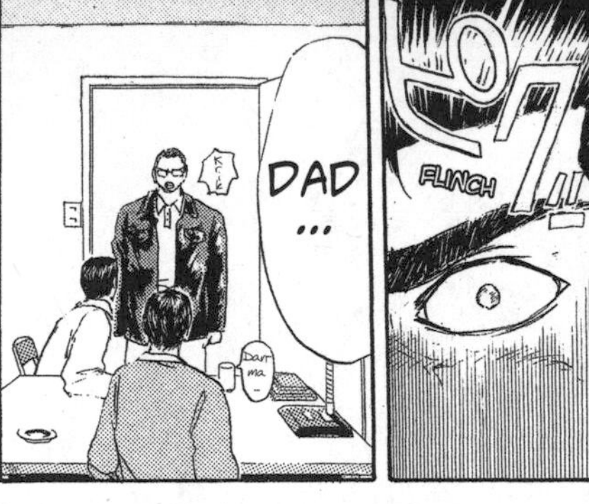
FLINCH
DAD ...

RYU-JI...
HON-ESTLY, YOU...

WHAT ARE YOU HERE FOR?
THAT'S NO WAY TO TALK TO YOUR FATHER !

Clink
THUP

WHAT'S THIS?

AN APART-MENT KEY AND SOME MONEY TO SET UP.
IT SHOULD BE ENOUGH FOR HALF A YEAR.

TO PUT IT SIMPLY, YOU'RE A PAIN IN MY ASS! JUST THE FACT THAT YOU'RE AROUND!
DON'T EVER COME BACK TO MY HOUSE!

FROM NOW ON, YOU'RE NOT MY CHILD! YOU'RE NOTHING TO ME!
YOU'RE DEAD TO THE DANMA FAMILY!
...
DO YOU HEAR ME?!
HEY, DANMA... AREN'T YOU GOING A LITTLE TOO FAR?
HEH! FINE WITH ME.
YOU'VE BEEN DEAD TO ME
FOR A LONG TIME NOW.
SLAP

I SWEAR, YOU DAMN PUNK!
DANMA, CALM DOWN!!
I DON'T EVER WANT TO SEE YOUR FACE AGAIN! DO YOU UNDER-STAND ME?!
... IDIOT.

OH!

RYUJI ...

WERE YOU OKAY? THEY DIDN'T DO ANYTHING HORRIBLE, DID THEY?
...
I'M SORRY. IT'S BECAUSE OF MY DAD
THAT ALL OF THIS HAP-PENED.

...
SO IT'S REALLY GONE ...
IT LOOKS LIKE I'M ALREADY SET TO CHANGE SCHOOLS ...
YOU KNOW THAT PRIVATE ONE IN HIRA-TSUKA ?

I'M GOING THERE STARTING NEXT WEEK.

...

I WONDER WHAT'S GOING TO HAPPEN TO US?

I CAN'T STAND BEING YANKED APART LIKE THIS.

ZAKK

D-DAD ...
...

YOU'RE DANMA, RIGHT?
DON'T EVER HAVE ANYTHING TO DO WITH MY DAUGHTER AGAIN.

DON'T BRING ANY MORE UNHAPPINESS TO MY CHILD!
DAD ?!

WE'RE GO-ING.
NO, LET GO OF ME!
RYUJI!

...
BRRRMMM

NAGISA. DO YOU UNDER-STAND ?
DON'T MEET THAT BOY EVER AGAIN!

DO YOU HAVE ANY IDEA HOW MUCH YOUR FATHER AND I WORRIED ABOUT YOU DURING THE THREE MONTHS YOU WERE GONE?

PLEASE ...
...
DON'T MAKE US WORRY ANY-MORE.

I'M SORRY, RYUJI.

YOU'RE NOW THE HEEL 'CAUSE OF ME.

POP POP POP !!!

HM ?
FWOOO

FWMMMMMMM
Ryuji!!

HIM ?!
NAGISAAAA!!
FWW MMM
SKR
SKREEE
RYUJI!!
GET ON!
HUH ?
GET ON !!
...
HEY!! WHAT ARE YOU DOING WITH NAGISA, YOU BASTARD ?!!!
DSHHH
Grrt

WHAT ARE YOU THINKING OF DOING, RYUJI?!
COME ON! THIS IS ...
LET'S RUN AWAY.
WHAT ?

LET'S RUN AWAY TO SOME PLACE FAR AWAY
AND LIVE TOGE-THER!

IF WE CAN'T FIND A ROOM TO RENT
I DON'T MIND A LIVE-IN JOB.

I DON'T CARE IF I'M SEEN AS A BAD GUY!

I'M JUST SICK OF THIS.
SICK OF THIS TOWN, SICK OF ADULTS ...

RYUJI ...

I WANT TO BE FREER !!

LET'S RUN AWAY
FROM THIS TOWN.

THERE'S NO PLACE IN THIS TOWN
FOR US ANYMORE.

LET'S FIND IT.

THE TWO OF US —

A TOWN WITHOUT ANNOYING ADULTS,

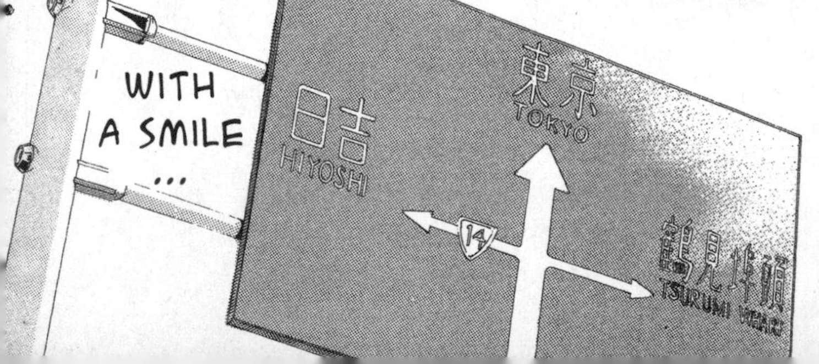
A TOWN THAT WILL TAKE US IN
WITH A SMILE ...
東京
TOKYO
日吉
HIYOSHI
14
鶴見埠頭
TSURUMI

A TOWN THAT'LL GRANT US FREEDOM.
...
STOP ...
...
SKRR

DWOOM
DWOOM

LET'S GO BACK TO OUR TOWN.
TO SHO-NAN ...

NO TOWN WILL GRANT OUR FREE-DOM.
IT DOESN'T MATTER WHERE WE RUN TO.

NO MATTER WHERE WE GO, THERE ARE GOING TO BE ADULTS

AND THEIR RULES.

IF WE RUN FROM THAT,
I FEAR WE'LL NEVER BE FREE.

...

I SEE ...

IT'S NOT LIKE ME
TO RUN AWAY, IS IT?

PLOP
PLOP

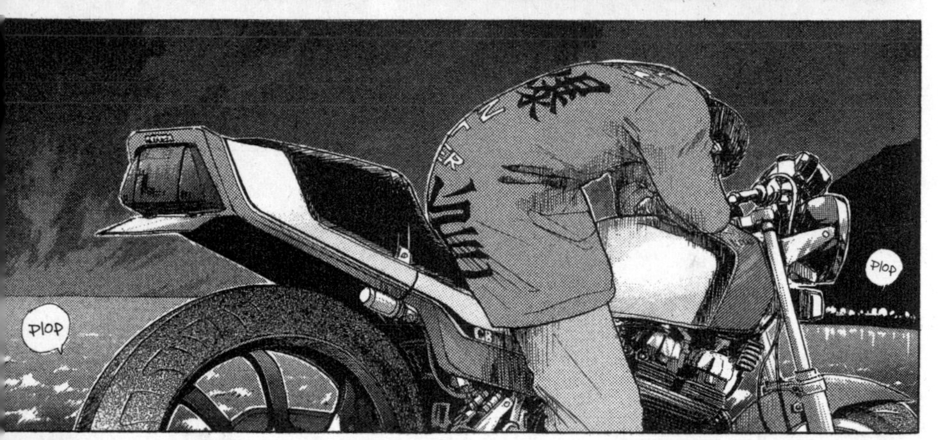
PLOP
PLOP

FWOM MM
SKRR
EI-KICHI...
...
DOOM
PAT
WHAT'RE YOU LOOKING SO DOWN FOR?

SO YOU GOT THROWN OUT OF YOUR HOUSE?

I GOT A CALL FROM NAGISA.
SHE'S WORRIED ABOUT YOU, SO SHE SENT ME.

WHAT'RE YOU GOING TO DO NOW?
NO-WHERE TO GO, HUH?

...

WANT TO COME
TO MY PLACE?

HUH?

WELL, IT'S A LITTLE CRAMPED, BUT THE MORE THE MERRIER!
I'M CHARGING YOU FOR FOOD, THOUGH.

...
DON'T WORRY ABOUT ME, EI-KICHI.

I CAN TAKE CARE OF OLD ME.
IF HAVE TO, I CAN GO TO TOKYO ALONE ...

BONK
THUD
TSK
WHAT THE HELL ARE YOU DOING?!
IDIOT!
DON'T ACT SHY
AROUND YOUR BOYS.
FINE, THEN. JUST FOR NOW.

CARE TO BAG SOME BOOZE ON THE WAY ?

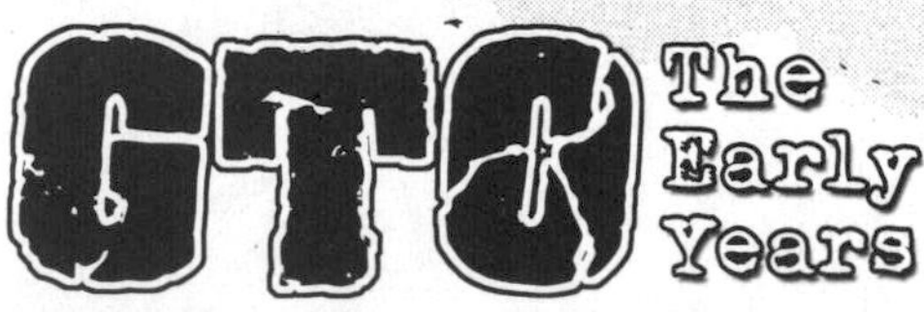


## Chapter 212:
## THE GREAT PART-TIME PLAN

OOH, IT'S COLD!
カチャ
CLINK
One CUP 横綱
One CUP 横綱
LET'S HURRY AND GET IN MY ROOM SO WE CAN POLISH OFF SOME HOT SAKE!
IS IT REALLY OKAY FOR ME TO TUMBLE IN?
Chew
YOUR MOM'S AROUND, RIGHT?
NO PROBLEM! WHEN I TOLD HER ABOUT YOUR DAD, SHE SAID, "AN AWFUL PERSON LIKE THAT HAS NO RIGHT TO BE A FATHER!"
Chomp
SHE WAS FIRED UP!
SORRY...
I'VE BEEN NOTHING BUT A BURDEN ON YOU.
WHAT ARE YOU SAYING, STUPID?
WE'RE BUDS, AREN'T WE?
CLICK
I'm home!
Excuse me!

I'M FEELING KINDA NERVOUS!
WHAT'RE YOU TALKING ABOUT? STOP WORRYING ABOUT IT AND JUST MAKE YOURSELF AT HOME!
At home, okay?
I HAVE A ROOM READY FOR YOU.
バン
SLAM
F-FOR REAL?

SEE? RIGHT HERE.
SLIDE
OH, HERE?
WELL, USE IT HOW-EVER YOU WANT.
This is your room from today.
HEY, THANK YOU.

LET ME KNOW IF ANY-THING COMES UP!
S-SURE!
Haha ha...
TUNK
?

BAM
...
...
...
SO, HOW'S **your room** ?
RATTLE
PRETTY NEAT, HUH?
BROK
SHONAN STREET PERFORM
SHONAN STREET STREET PERFORM

WH- WHAT'S THE DEAL?!
Shake
Shake
YOU CALL THAT A ROOM?

SHAKE
SHAKE
It's just a closet!

THAT'S RIGHT, IT'S A CLOSET! YOU GOT A PRO-BLEM WITH THAT?
YOU'D THROW A BUD INTO SOME HOLE IN THE GROUND?
Huh?!
This is my room.
Shp

RATTLE
HERE
RIGHT, YOU HAVE THIS CAN SPACE TOO, SO CHILL.

Woof woof
...

BRING IT ON! I'LL TAKE YOUR ROOM BY FORCE, THEN!
Shaaaaah
Lion's tough, yo.

SHUT UP! IF YOU'RE RIGHT NEXT TO ME, I WON'T EVEN BE ABLE TO BEAT OFF IN PRIVATE!
No way, Shun's time has come!
WHAT'D YOU SAY, PUNK?
Bam
Bam

ARE YOU TRYING TO MESS WITH ME?!
SHUT UP! A FREE-LOADER LIKE YOU SHOULDN'T BITCH!
HUH? YOU WANNA FIGHT?!
HUH?
GRAAAH

SHUT UP!
BAM

FOR GOODNESS' SAKE, WHAT TIME DO YOU THINK IT IS?
IF YOU'RE GOING TO FIGHT, THEN I'LL DECIDE FOR YOU. Me!
Twitch
Oh, good evening.
YOU'RE ACTING LIKE KIDS! ALL YOU'RE TRYING TO DO IS SPLIT A ROOM!
SHUT UP!
KEEP OUT OF THIS, HAG!
GRIND
WHO THE HELL DO YOU THINK YOU'RE TALKING TO?
HOOK
...
...

IF YOU'RE GOING TO BE A BAD-TEMPERED BRAT ABOUT IT THEN THIS IS ALL THE SPACE YOU'RE GETTING!
BRIIIIP
Heave-ho
Heave-ho
Hup hup
okay, everything right of this line is your room.
Rip rip
...
WHAAA?!

NOW, YOU CAN USE THIS PART OF THE ROOM, RYUJI.
Here, you can use this bed.
Been— through a lot? Think of this as your home now.
Jeez, I'm really sorry for all of this.
HEY, WHAT THE HELL IS UP WITH THIS DIVISION, HAG?
YOU KNOW, YOU'RE QUITE A DISH, RYUJI.
Ha ha ha ha ha
I'd never be able to tell that you're a mother, yourself!
Oh yeah? wanna be my bed?
Oh honestly—
CAN'T YOU HEAR ME? LISTEN, HAG!
HA-AAG!

BAZONK

I'M THE LADY OF THIS HOUSE.
IF YOU'VE GOT A COMPLAINT, MAKE IT ONCE YOU'VE EARNED YOUR FAIR SHARE.

I'LL ALSO MAKE SURE TO PAY YOU FROM WHAT I MAKE.
Hahahahaha
OH, DON'T WORRY ABOUT IT, RYUJI! YOU'RE JUST STAYING HERE.
...

I'LL BECOME A DELINQUENT!
You already are one.
I'LL WRITE IN TO A DAYTIME TV SHOW ABOUT MY HORRIBLE MOTHER WHO ONLY GIVES HER REAL SON 10 SQUARE FEET TO LIVE IN!
Can you even write?

Ha ha ha ha
Ho ho ho
...

ALL RIGHT, FINE THEN! I WILL GO OUT AND MAKE SOME MONEY!!
YOU GREEDY HAG!!

BGRAK
I CAN MAKE MONEY ANY TIME I WANT, YOU OLD HAG!
THUDT
BANG
URAAAAAAAAAGH
BRSHHT
Who's an old hag?! You should be calling me "sis"!!
Sis, my ass! Don't go blabbing when you've got tar-black areolae...
What'd you say, you prepuced...
Strong... Definitely Eikichi's mom...
...

UH!
SPACIOUS
THAT STUPID OLD HAG PISSES ME OFF.
CRAMP
RYUJI
EIKICHI: DO NOT ENTER
STUPID EIKICHI
I SWEAR, WHEN SHE GETS OLD, I'M GONNA DUMP HER ON SOME MOUNTAIN!

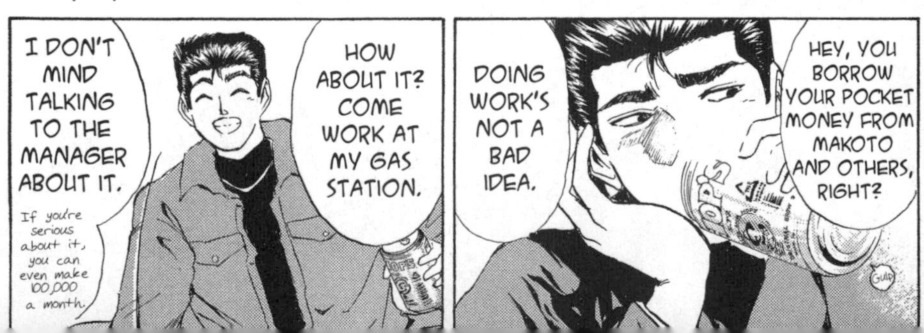
HEY, YOU BORROW YOUR POCKET MONEY FROM MAKOTO AND OTHERS, RIGHT?
DOING WORK'S NOT A BAD IDEA.
GULP
HOW ABOUT IT? COME WORK AT MY GAS STATION.
I DON'T MIND TALKING TO THE MANAGER ABOUT IT.
If you're serious about it, you can even make 100,000 a month.

RYUJI
BOYS HAVE GOT TO HELP EACH OTHER OUT!
YOU ...
YOU REALLY ARE A GOOD GUY.

AND A GOOD GUY WOULD GIVE UP A LITTLE ROOM, LIKE THIS ...
SLIDE

NO... THIS AND THAT ARE TWO COMPLETELY DIFFERENT THINGS.
SLIDE

WE'RE BOYS, RIGHT? THEN GIVE ME JUST THIS MUCH...
SHUT UP! WE'RE NOT BOYS JUST WHEN IT SUITS YOU!
SLIDE

WHAT DO YOU MEAN? YOU'RE THE REASON FOR ALL OF THIS!
WHAT'S THAT? I HAVE YOUR MOM'S PERMISSION ...
DON'T ACT FRESH JUST BECAUSE YOU'VE SUCKED UP TO A HAG!
YOU WANNA GO? HUH?
BRING IT ON, PUNK!
Shut uuup!
YOU damn kids!

DOMO
STATION
THANK YOU VERY MUCH!!
ブロロ..
BRRMMM

PHEW! SWEAT OF MY BROW, HUH?
Not like when I beat off.
OH!
WEL-COME!!
THAT'S ONIZUKA, THE NEW PART-TIMER YOU BROUGHT IN?
HE'S QUITE THE HARD WORK-ER!
A great refer-ral!
AH, YOU THINK?
HAHA
DOMO station

HEHEH ... OF COURSE I AM!
IF I REALLY TRY, A PART-TIME JOB OR TWO IS NOTHING.
SCRUB
SCRUB
JUST YOU WATCH, HAG. I'LL MAKE A BUNCH OF MONEY FAST
SCRUB
AND SLAP YOU IN YOUR FACE WITH A STACK OF BILLS WHILE YOU LICK MY FEET!
SCRUB
SKRR SKRRRR
HUH?
WEL-COME!
WHAT'S WITH THAT HAIR OF YOURS? AREN'T YOU A STAFFER?
IS THAT HOW YOU PRESENT YOURSELF TO CUS-TOMERS?
HEY, GET ME YOUR MAN-AGER.
Well, you say so, but...
GET HIM, I SAID!
HAH?
ANYTHING WRONG?
HM? OH, THIS CUSTOMER WAS JUST TRYING TO TAKE ME ON...

TAKE YOU ON?
HEY, KID! WHO'RE YOU TALKING TO?

YOU!

WHAT DID YOU SAY??
HAH?
ONI-ZUKA!!

I'M SORRY OUR STAFF HAS BEEN RUDE TO YOU...
Huh?
JUST HOW THE HELL DO YOU TRAIN THEM?
Bugs me to hell...
Want me to complain to your head office?

I-I'M SORRY. HOW CAN I MAKE THIS UP TO YOU?
You apologize, too!
B-But, he's the one who...
IT DOESN'T MAT-TER!

YOU THINK I'LL BE HAPPY WITH JUST AN APOLOGY?
UHM, WHAT DO YOU WANT ME TO...

YEAH...
WELL, TO START...

How about you make this guy fix his hair
into a 7-3 part.

A 7-3 PART ??
BOSS, GIVE ME THE WORD AND I'LL KILL HIM.
I MEAN, THIS PIECE OF GARBAGE WANTS TO MAKE ME GET A 7-3 PART...
WHAT ?
DO IT.
IF YOU DON'T, YOU'RE FIRED !!!
...
じゃーーん
TA-DAAAA
Eikichi
Quiver
Quiver
...
...
GYAHA-HAHAHA !
LOOKS GREAT ON YOU!!
THAT'S GREAT! KEEP UP THE HARD WORK HERE WITH THAT HAIRSTYLE, KID! AHAHA-HAHAHA!
Y-YOU SIDE-BURNED MONKEY ...
E-EIKICHI, YOU IDIOT! HOLD IT IN! IF YOU GET PISSED NOW, YOU'RE FINISHED!
SHAKE
H-HE'S RIGHT ...
IF THIS IS ALL IT TAKES FOR ME TO GET PISSED OFF, THEN I'LL NEVER HEAR THE END OF IT FROM THAT HAG!

HOLD IT IN, AND SOME DAY I'LL BE FREE!

YOU BETTER BE CAREFUL. THE CUSTOMER IS ALWAYS RIGHT, YOU KNOW.
WELL, I SEE YOUR SINCERITY, SO I'LL LET YOU OFF WITH THIS TODAY.
PAT

OH, YES ...
CLICK

THROW THIS GUM AWAY FOR ME.
POP

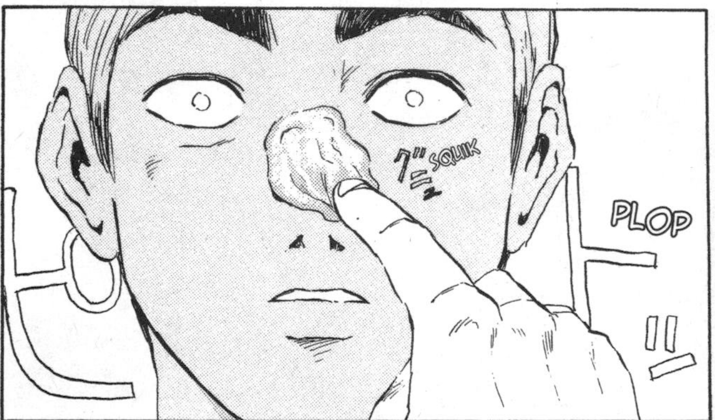
SQUIK
PLOP

Phew! Now things will be peaceful here once again.
?!

GYA-HAHA! WORK HARD, BOY!
BEEP
...

That piece of shit!!
STRETCH

GRAB
DON'T EVER COME BACK, YOU DUMBASS!
HURL
SMASH
Slar
Skree-eee
GWMMMMMMMMM

SKR
SCRUB
...
SCRUB
SCRUB

YOU THREW A
STONE, DIDN'T YOU?

WH-
WHAT DO YOU MEAN?
SCRUB
SCRUB

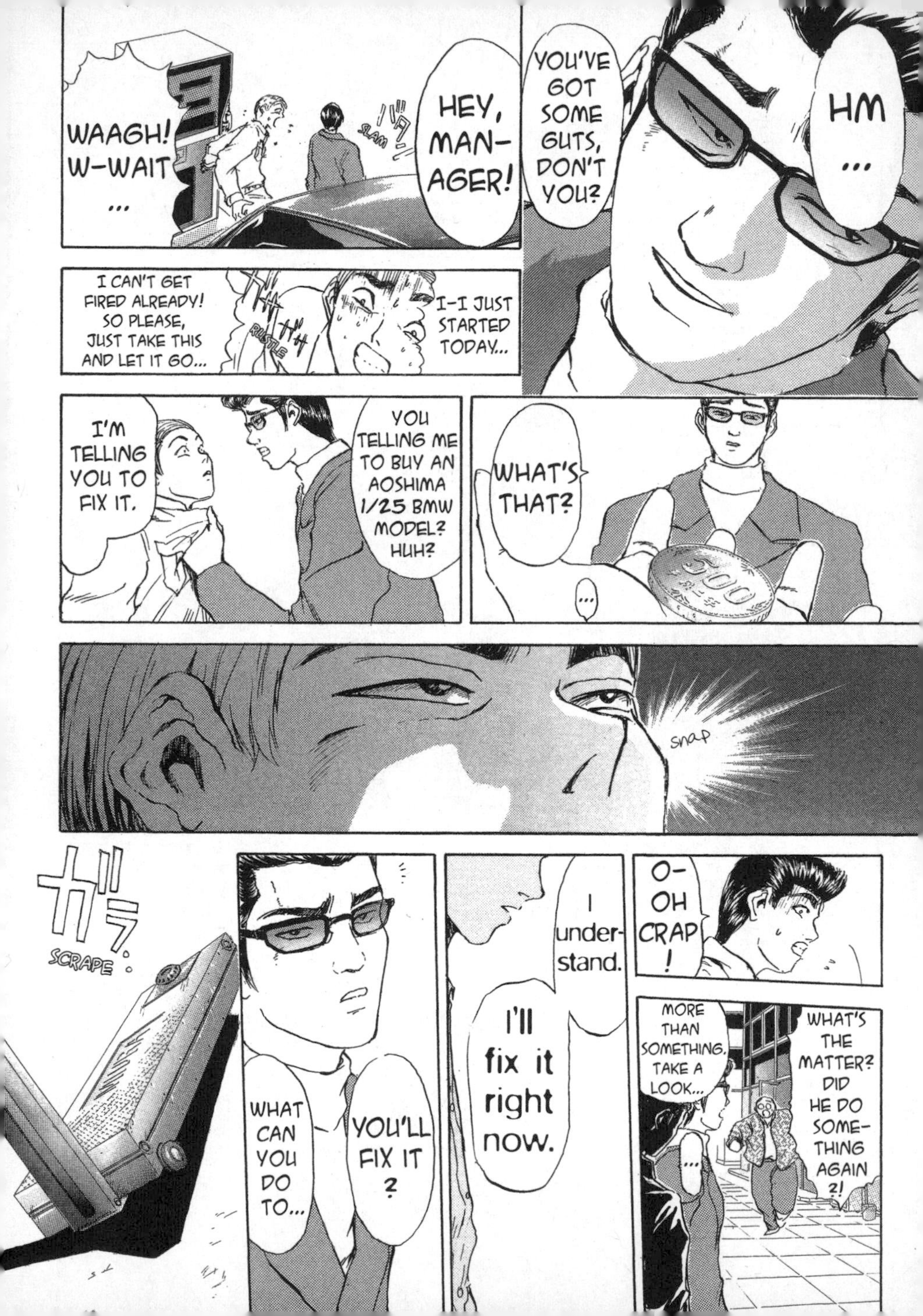
HM ...
YOU'VE GOT SOME GUTS, DON'T YOU?
HEY, MAN-AGER!
SLAM
WAAGH! W-WAIT ...
I-I JUST STARTED TODAY...
RUSTLE
I CAN'T GET FIRED ALREADY! SO PLEASE, JUST TAKE THIS AND LET IT GO...
WHAT'S THAT?
...
YOU TELLING ME TO BUY AN AOSHIMA 1/25 BMW MODEL? HUH?
I'M TELLING YOU TO FIX IT.
snap
O-OH CRAP!
WHAT'S THE MATTER? DID HE DO SOME-THING AGAIN?!
MORE THAN SOMETHING, TAKE A LOOK...
...
I understand.
I'll fix it right now.
YOU'LL FIX IT?
WHAT CAN YOU DO TO...
SCRAPE

BSHHH

?!

WH-WHAT ARE YOU DOING?! STOP IT!!
MAN-AGER! DON'T JUST STAND THERE, STOP HIM ...
Oh, this needs some work too!
BAM
THUDT
Eek! Stop!

GRAB

THE MAN-AGER?
I DON'T CARE WHO!
GSHT

Snap
Snap
SNAP
'Cause I think I just quit working here.

?!

COME ON, WHERE SHOULD I FIX NEXT?
S-STOP, EIKICHI! HEY!!
GCHT
THOK

I BEG YOU, SIR, FORGIVE HIM!
I'LL FIX IT GOOD!!
Eek!! Please stop!
I'LL STOP HIM RIGHT NOW!
...
FIRED ...
WAIT! ANYTHING BUT THAT!
I-I'LL MAKE THIS RIGHT ...!
HEY, EIKICHI! STO-OOP!
URYAGH!
Stop it! Eek!
YOU TOO.
...
You're fired
too.
FIRED?
I'M FIRED?
Nod
Fired?
I'm fired too?
Nod Nod

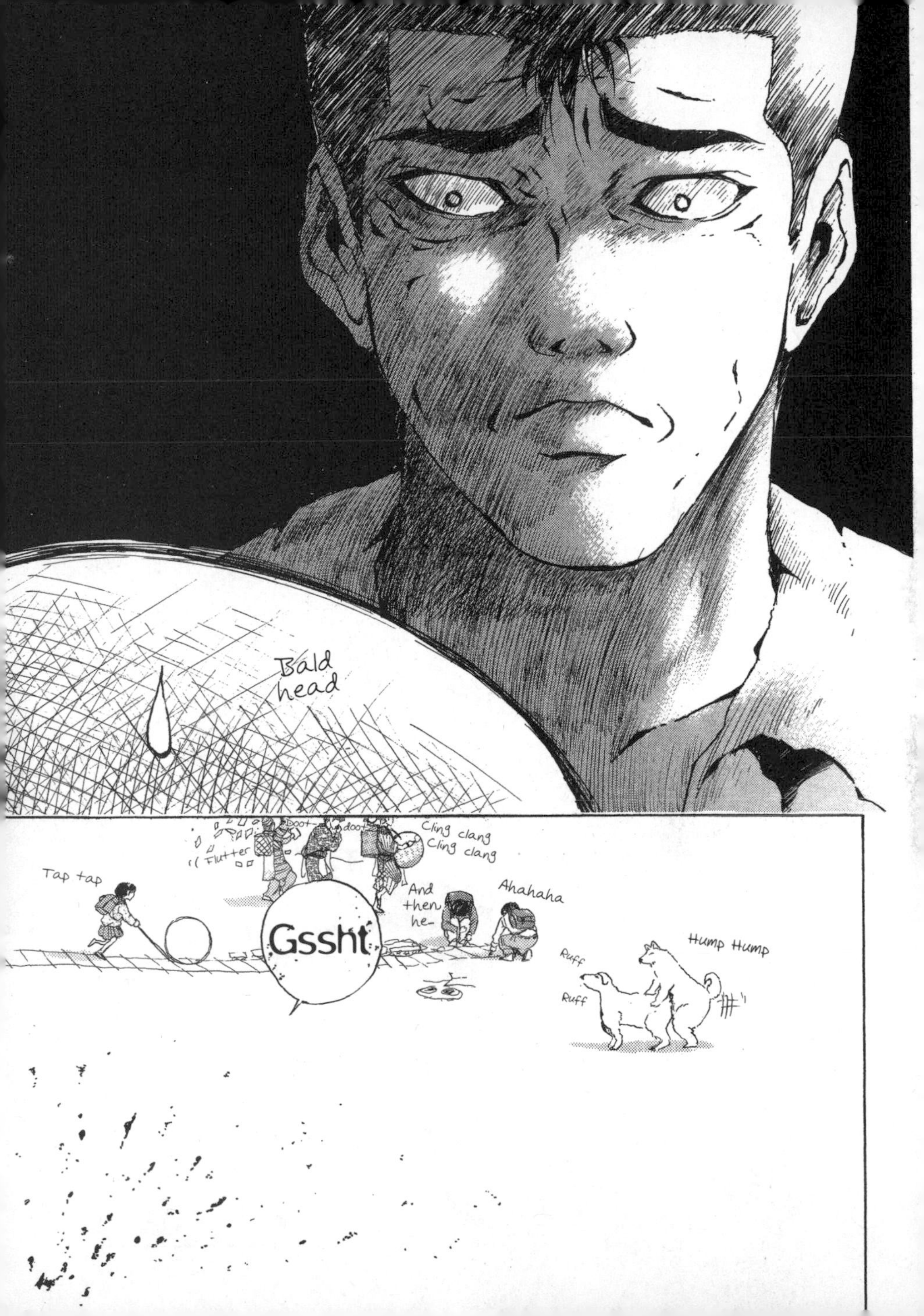
Bald head
Flutter
Doot-doot
Cling clang
Cling clang
Tap tap
And then he-
Ahahaha
Gssht
Hump Hump
Ruff
Ruff

BAZONK

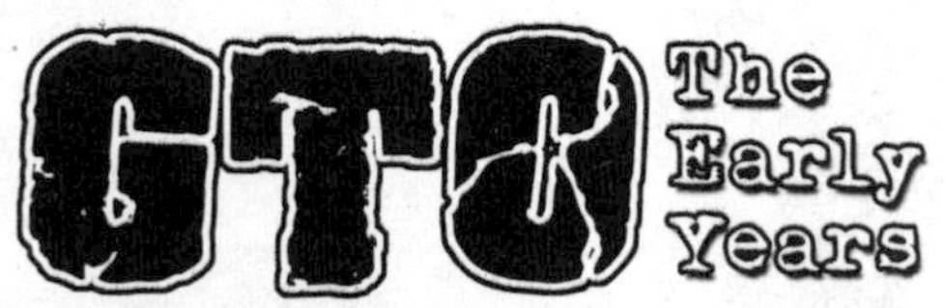


## Chapter 213: THE STRANGEST PART-TIME JOB

YARGH! PISSES ME OFF!
TO BE HONEST, I STILL HADN'T FOUND A PART-TIME JOB THAT I COULD HOLD DOWN FOR LONG.
I'M NEVER GOING BACK TO WORK THAT CRAP JOB!
THAT MADE TWENTY...
Keh
I'D QUIT EVERY TIME OVER A FIGHT.
I NEVER FELT LIKE MY FISTS WERE CURSED QUITE LIKE TODAY. YEAH... IT WAS ALL BECAUSE I'M TOO STRONG.
I BEGAN TO FRET.
EVER SINCE THEN, MOM TREATED ME LIKE SOME PARASITE.
Here you go, Ryuji! Sea bream!
Oh you're always so kind.
SHAKE
RYUJI HAD LONG STARTED WORKING AT MR. KAKIUCHI'S BIKE SHOP.
IT WAS ON SUCH A COLD AFTERNOON, ENOUGH TO CHILL YOUR BODY AND HEART,
THAT I CAME ACROSS THAT JOB...
HEY, YOU ...

Care to try your hand at
kid-nap-ping?
...
STEP STEP
スタ スタ
...
HAAH... AREN'T THERE ANY GOOD JOBS AROUND?
SOMETHING WHERE YOU CAN JUST MAKE A BUNCH OF MONEY FAST?
As if!
HM?
30,000 A DAY?
Seriously?
HIGH-PAYING PART-TIME JOB
高給アルバ
DETAILS GIVEN ON-SITE
委細面談
K企画
K PLANNING
030-
WHAT'S THIS? LOOKS KIND OF FISHY...
ISN'T THIS PHONE NUMBER A CELL NUMBER, TOO?
No clue what kind of work it is...
...

WELL, IT'S NOT LIKE I HAVE OTHER LEADS.
IT DOES SAY "HIGH-PAYING," TOO.
I'LL AT LEAST GIVE THEM A CALL. WHAT DO I HAVE TO LOSE?
高給で
BEEP BOOP BAP BOOP BEEP
Brrrrr- Click
HI, I'M CALLING ABOUT THE PART-TIME JOB.
OH, YOU'RE INTERESTED IN THE PART-TIME POSITION?
Please wait a moment.
KNOCK KNOCK
...
ひとさらい やりませんか 高給優遇
CARE TO TRY YOUR HAND AT KIDNAPPING? HIGH PAY, GOOD BENEFITS
YES, HELLO? MY NAME IS OHITO, I'M IN CHARGE OF IT.
OH, HELLO. I SAW THIS FLIER FOR A HIGH-PAYING JOB, IS IT FOR REAL?
YES.
I'D SAY IT PAYS ABOUT 30,000 A DAY.
It's not all that high-paying, I suppose... Hahaha!
WHA?
TH-THIRTY THOUSAND?!
That's 300,000 in ten days!!
WELL, PLEASE STOP BY TO CHECK IT OUT.
WHERE ARE YOU RIGHT NOW?
OH, I'M ON X STREET, IN THE PHONE BOOTH RIGHT NEXT TO THE KIMONO STORE.
IN THAT CASE, WE'RE RIGHT BY YOU.
LOOK RIGHT BEHIND YOU.

HUH?
大村ビル
...
DING
12345
WHUM
THIS PLACE IS CLEANER THAN I THOUGHT IT'D BE.
AT LEAST THE BUILDING ITSELF DOESN'T LOOK THAT SKETCHY.
WELCOME!
OH♡
cute!
I'M HERE ABOUT THE PART-TIME JOB...
AH, THE ONE WHO JUST CALLED. PLEASE, COME THIS WAY.
SIR, THIS IS THE INDIVIDUAL WHO WAS ASKING ABOUT THE PART-TIME JOB...
WAIT ONE SECOND, I'M ON THE PHONE.

SO IT SEEMS LIKE A PROPER COMPANY.
I GUESS ADS ON LIGHT POLES AREN'T TOTALLY WORTHLESS AFTER ALL!
BOSE
THANK YOU FOR WAIT-ING.
ZAKK
?!
GRIN
I'm the sales manager, Yoshio Ohito.
HM... SO YOU'RE A HIGH SCHOOL STUDENT?
WELL, I SUPPOSE THAT'S FINE. IT'S A SIMPLE JOB, AFTER ALL.
...
GRIN
I CAN'T BELIEVE HOW OFF THAT HAIRSTYLE LOOKS ON HIM.
I-I GOTTA BAD FEELING...

SIR
You have a phone call.
Grin
I'LL BE RIGHT THERE.
...
WELL, THEN ...
SCOOT
WHY DON'T WE GET YOU STARTED TODAY.
OUR ACCOUNTING IS CLEAN SO DON'T WORRY.
O-Okay. It's like a clip joint...
HM?
BUH ??
OKAY, THE ROOM RIGHT OVER HERE.
Hey, Kashiwagi! It's that room...
BONK
SLAM
...
U-UM... I HAVE A QUESTION ...

Hahahaha
WHAT EXACTLY DOES THIS COMPANY DO?
It's just a part-time job, but I feel like I should ask...
TWITCH
That's not something you need to know.
Just do the jobs we tell you to do.
Keheheh
GRIN
That's all there is to it.
Now, get started.
...
OKAY, READY?
FWAP
JUST CUT OUT LETTERS FROM THESE NEWSPAPERS
AND PUT THEM IN THIS BOX IN ORDER.
You don't need to organize by size.
THAT'S IT?
YEP!
Do your best!
WOW, THAT'S EASY.
OKAY, LIKE THIS...
CLIP
I THOUGHT THEY'D MAKE ME DO SCARY STUFF!
IF I CAN MAKE 30,000 A DAY DOING THIS, I LUCKED OUT!
CLIP

OKAY, DONE!
BUT WHAT COULD THEY USE THESE FOR?
HAHAHA! MAN, THIS IS A PIECE OF CAKE!
I MEAN, IF YOU LINE THEM UP LIKE THIS...
Voilà, a black-mail letter ♡
...
Ha ha ha...
WE HAVE YOUR DAUGHTER. IF YOU WANT HER BACK, HAVE 5 MILLION YEN READY.
KLAK
ARE YOU DONE?
OH! Y-Y-YES!
ARE YOU SURE I SHOULD GET PAID 30,000 FOR THIS?
This work is...
DON'T WORRY, THE PROFIT WILL BE HUGE!
SHHT
HUGE?
Just using some letters?
SERIOUS-LY, WHAT EXACTLY DOES THIS COMPANY DO?

I SHOULD ASK THE MANAGER, BUT HE SEEMS BUSY...
...
DO YOU REALLY WANT TO KNOW?
If I tell you ...
you might not be able to ever leave.
WH-WHAT DO YOU MEAN BY THAT?!
I'M JUST JOK-ING. Joke!
HM?
?!
A-ARE THOSE REDDISH BLACK DOTS FROM
SHADY INJEC-TIONS ?!?!
OKAY, I'LL GO GET THE MANAG-ER.
U-UM ... WAIT ...
KLAK
WHAT IN THE WORLD DOES THIS COMPANY DO?!
AAAA-AGH! I NEED TO KNOW !!
KREE

?!
SLAM
KLAK
OH MY. THANK YOU FOR WAITING!
You were rather fast!
Haha haha ha
I-I JUST SAW A MAN COVERED IN BLOOD IN THERE! HELP HIM!!
COVERED IN BLOOD? WHAT IS THIS?
THERE WAS NO SUCH MAN THERE.
BUT I'M SURE THAT I JUST ...
You must be imagining things.

HERE YOU GO.
TAKE THIS AND GO TO THE YAMASHITA PARK ENTRANCE.
...
WHAT?
ALL YOU NEED TO DO IS STAND AT THE ENTRANCE.
When I give the signal
raise your hand and make a V-sign.
HUH?
OH, BY THE WAY, YOU DIDN'T GO IN THAT ROOM, DID YOU?
HALT
THAT ROOM OVER THERE.
立入禁止
NO ENTRY
WHA? UM...
A V-SIGN, OKAY?
Good luck!
Hahaha
UM... WHAT FOR?
Entering that room is forbidden.
Please don't go in, okay?

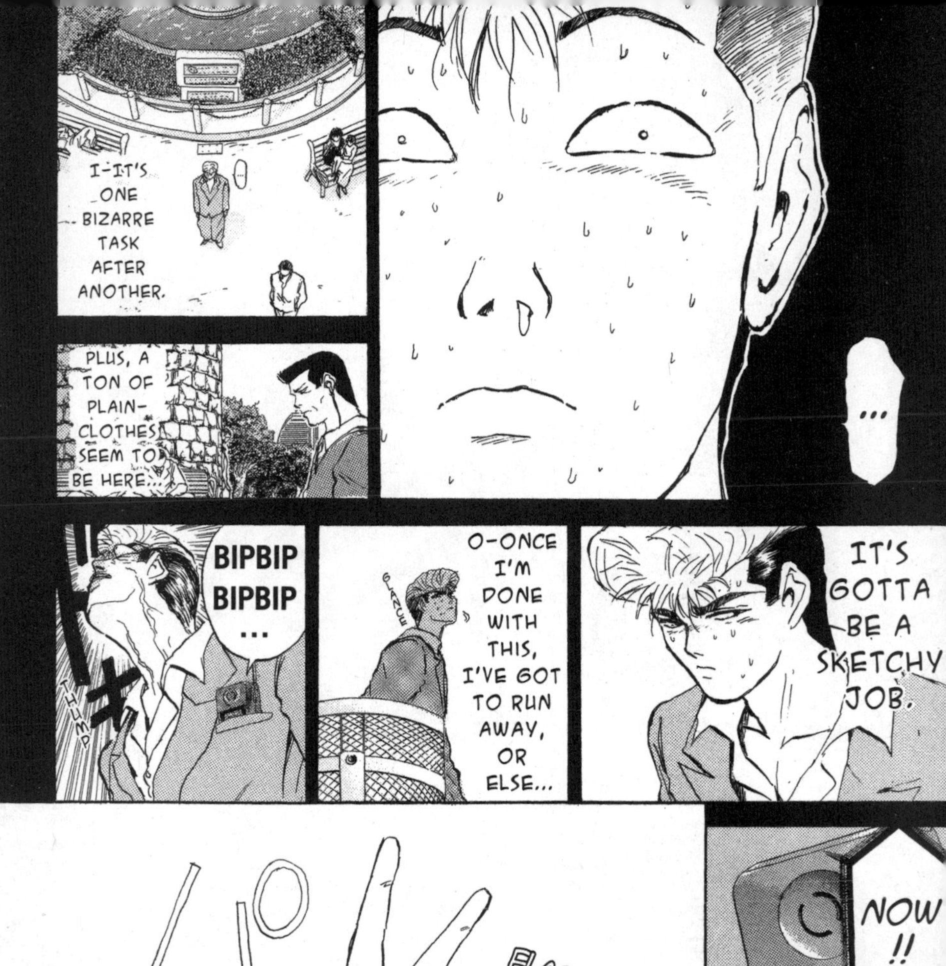
I-IT'S ONE BIZARRE TASK AFTER ANOTHER.
...
PLUS, A TON OF PLAIN-CLOTHES SEEM TO BE HERE...
...
BIPBIP BIPBIP ...
THUMP
GLANCE
O-ONCE I'M DONE WITH THIS, I'VE GOT TO RUN AWAY, OR ELSE...
IT'S GOTTA BE A SKETCHY JOB.

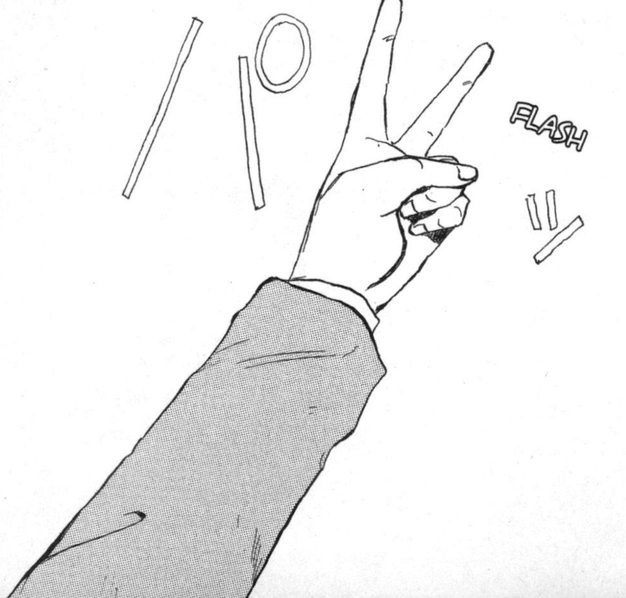
FLASH

NOW !!

AAAAGH!!
Who cares anymore!

...
...
...
...
...
...
...
GREAT WORK! PLEASE WAIT HERE...
SLAM
PFAH
HAAH
HAAH
HAAH
FINE, I'LL SEARCH THIS PLACE WHAT-EVER THE COST!
Don't mess with me.
CLICK
I FEEL LIKE I'M GOING TO GO CRAZY!
WHAT ARE THEY MAKING ME DO?
IF THIS IS ALL RELATED TO SOME CASE...
HMM?
I JUST SENSE SOME-THING...

SLAM
CRAP! THERE'S A LOOK-OUT!
DAMMIT! ARE THEY TRYING TO KEEP ME FROM RUNNING?
DON'T GO IN, OKAY?
THERE'S SOME SECRET IN HERE ...
KREAK
...
立入禁止
DANGER
...
GREEE
...
GGT
Dan ...
Gar ?
*No, Onizuka, "Danger"!

?!
PLAP
I-I DIDN'T SEE ANY-THING! I SWEAR ...
I SWEAR I DIDN'T SEE ANY-THING! WAA-AAGH!
Waaaagh!

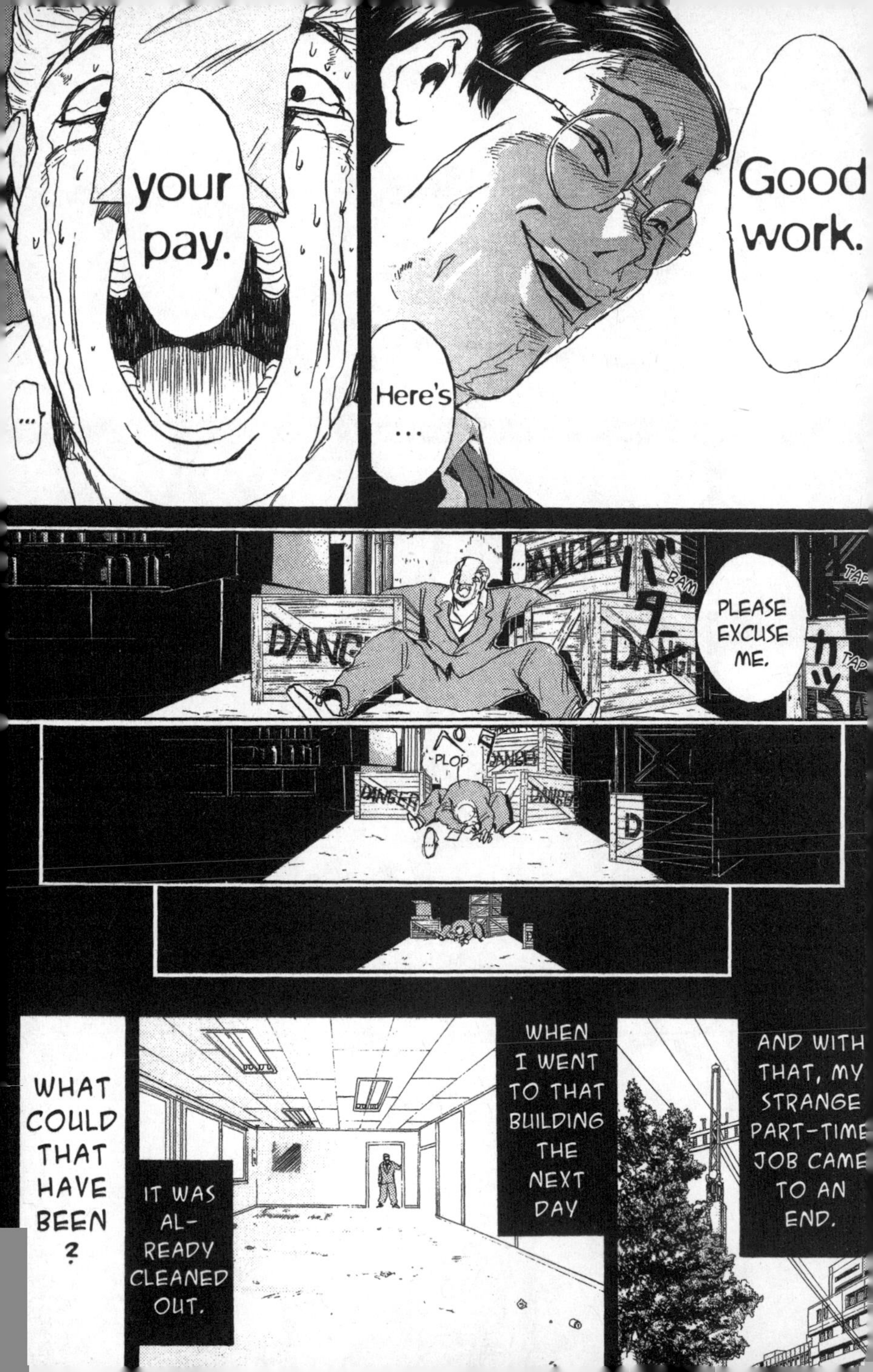
Good work.
Here's...
your pay.
...
TAP
TAP
PLEASE EXCUSE ME.
BAM
...
PLOP
AND WITH THAT, MY STRANGE PART-TIME JOB CAME TO AN END.
WHEN I WENT TO THAT BUILDING THE NEXT DAY
IT WAS AL-READY CLEANED OUT.
WHAT COULD THAT HAVE BEEN?

THAT GANG WITH THE SAME PARTED HAIR-STYLE ...
THE BLUE MARKS ON THAT LADY'S ARM ...
THE CONTENTS OF THOSE CARDBOARD BOXES ...
IT WAS ALL A MYSTERY.
EXCUSE ME.
Kid-nap-ping ...
Whoooo
...
ULTIMATELY, AFTER THAT DAY...
I NEVER FOUND A JOB I COULD HOLD DOWN
AND SO I CONTINUED TO LIVE IN SHAME AT HOME.
HM? SO THEY BUILT A PACHINKO PLACE HERE.
HMM, 800 AN HOUR?
DING
CLANK
PWEE
Give me more, give me more!
KWING
ROLL

WEL-COME!
UM, I'M HERE BECAUSE I SAW THE FLIER OUTSIDE ...
SO, YOU'RE INTER-ESTED IN A PART-TIME JOB?
PERFECT TIMING! WE HAVEN'T HAD MANY APPLI-CANTS.
I'm the owner of this store.
My name is Ohito.
ACTUALLY, WE HAVE A BETTER POSITION THAT PAYS 30,000 YEN A DAY...
ER, NO THANKS! S-SORRY FOR BOTHER-ING YOU!
STAMP
STAMP
Oh, hey! Wait!
Eek!
THAT'S RIGHT... EVEN IN JAPAN, YOU CAN FIND SOME OF THE STRANGEST PART-TIME JOBS...
PERHAPS EVEN IN YOUR TOWN.

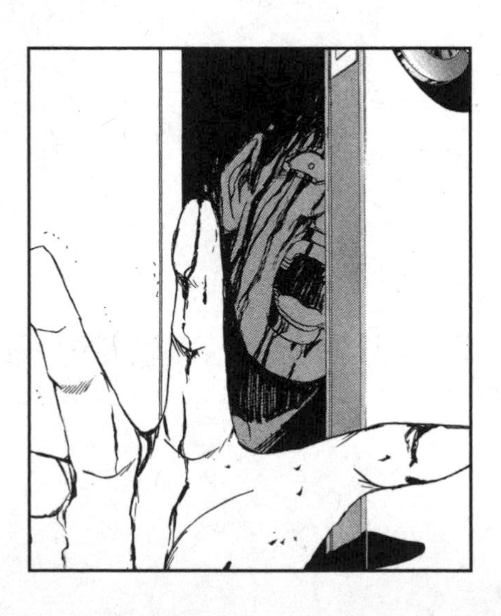

A MONTH HAD PASSED SINCE I COULDN'T SEE NAGISA ANYMORE.
MAKE-UP

I'D GONE TO HER HOUSE COUNTLESS TIMES, BUT THERE WAS NO WAY THEY'D LET ME.
THE DAYS PASSED AS WE MADE DO WITH SECRET PHONE CALLS FROM PUBLIC PHONES

愛
Squeak
LUV

AND EXCHANGING MESSAGES WRITTEN ON WINDOWS.
LUV YOU!

AND ONCE SHE STARTED GOING TO HER NEW SCHOOL

ACCOMPANIED BY A RELATIVE...

THE ONLY WAY NAGISA AND I COULD STAY CONNECTED
伝言板
WAS THROUGH BRIEF MESSAGES LEFT ON THE BOARD AT THE STATION.

GTO
The Early Years
Chapter 214: THE MAN WHO CAME FROM THE SEA

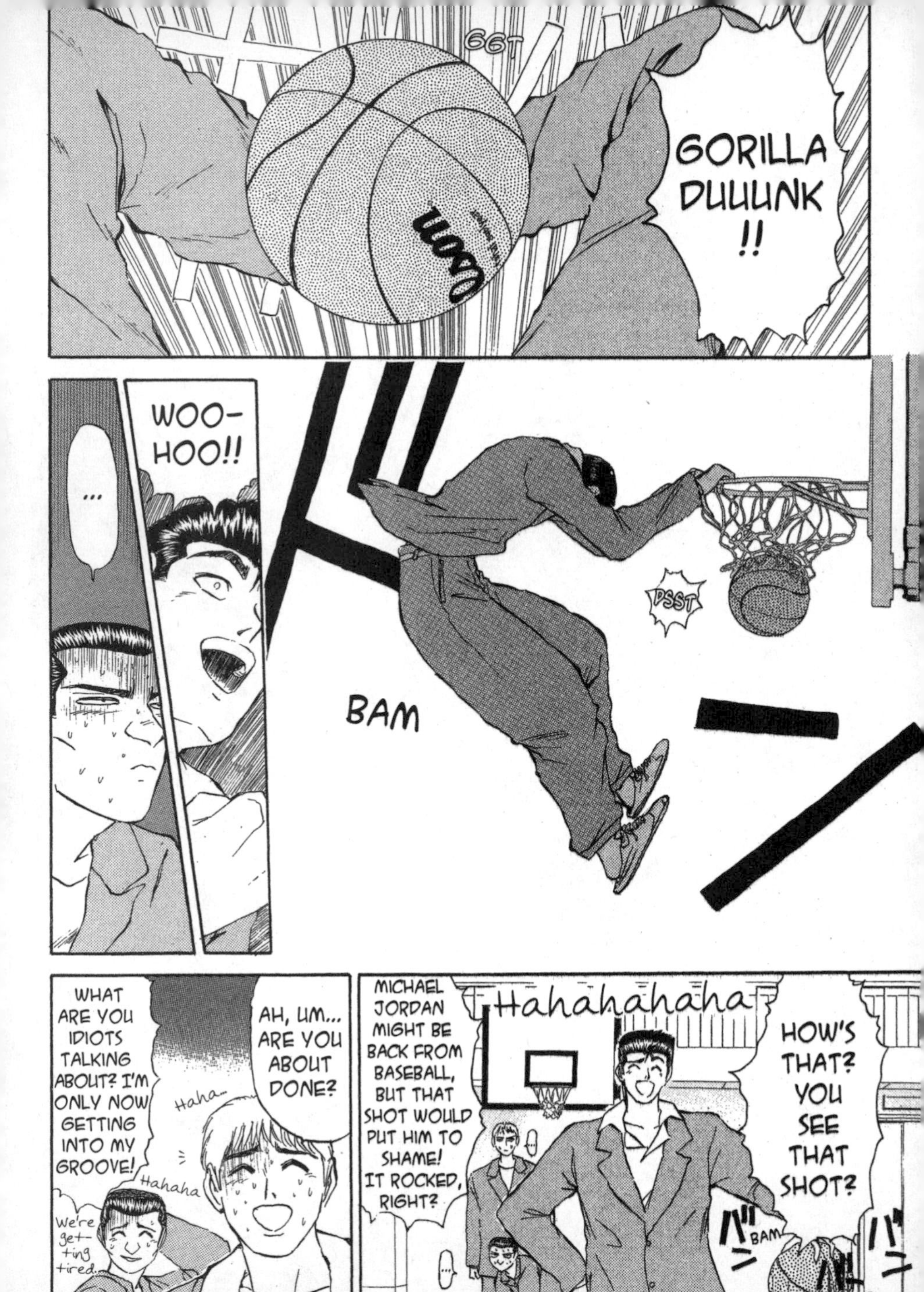

GORILLA DUUUNK !!
WOO-HOO!!
...
DSST
BAM
HOW'S THAT? YOU SEE THAT SHOT?
BAM
MICHAEL JORDAN MIGHT BE BACK FROM BASEBALL, BUT THAT SHOT WOULD PUT HIM TO SHAME! IT ROCKED, RIGHT?
Hahahahahaha
...
AH, UM... ARE YOU ABOUT DONE?
WHAT ARE YOU IDIOTS TALKING ABOUT? I'M ONLY NOW GETTING INTO MY GROOVE!
Haha...
Hahaha
We're get-ting tired...

...
OKAY, GET READY. I'M DOING ONE MORE.
TUMP
TUMP
Re-ally?
I'M GO-ING!
BOOM
SLAM DUNK!!
PSSHT
BNG
oof
...
AIR WALK INTO A...
BAM
BAM
ALL RIGHT, NOW I'M GETTING HEATED UP!
BAM
BAM
Hey!!
SEE, DIDN'T I TELL YOU, TSUKAI?
HE'S BEEN LIKE THIS FOR A WHILE NOW. HE CAN'T SEE NAGISA ANYMORE, YOU KNOW?
SO HE'S JUST RE-BOUNDED ON TO US.
It sucks bad.
YOU SAY SOME-THING, ATSUSHI?
Hm? Er, no...
ALL RIGHT, NEXT UP IS MY MIRACLE TRIPLE-DECKER SLAM DUNK!
YOU READY?
Hahahaha
BAM
BAM
...
You're terrible
YOU JOIN IN ON THE NEXT ONE.
WHAA?
THUD
OWWW!
Hmm, fail. Once more.
Whaaaa?!
TEE HEE

LOOKS LIKE RYUJI'S DOING PRETTY GOOD.
YEP!
HE MIGHT HAVE BECOME A LITTLE MEAN, THOUGH.
THEY'RE COMMUNICATING BY POSTING MESSAGES ON A BOARD, I HEARD?
Giggle
Like kids!
HOW NICE, LIKE MIDDLE SCHOOLERS OR SOMETHING...
Tee hee
I JUST WISH THEY'D GIVE NAGISA HER FREEDOM BACK.
Okay, next one!
BAM BAM
I SAW HER THE OTHER DAY AT THE STATION WITH... HER AUNT, I THINK.
SHE WAS STUCK TO NAGISA THE ENTIRE TIME. IT'S LIKE SHE'S UNDER HOUSE ARREST!
EH, MAYBE THAT'S HOW IT IS WHEN YOU'RE GROWING UP!
YEAH, MAYBE.
RIGHT?
IT'S NOT LIKE SHE DID ANYTHING WRONG.
HELD DOWN BY ADULTS' RULES...
DON'T WORRY, SHE WON'T LET IT BEAT HER.

THUD
TRYING TO ACT ALL COOL UP THERE, EIKICHI?
Hahahaha
You wanna shoot some, too? It feels great!
BAM
BAM
BAM
I-I BIT MY TONGUE...
Are you stupid or what?
SHAKE
SHAKE

TOILET
JEEZ ...
I'M LETTING HIM STAY IN MY ROOM BUT HE'S USING MORE OF IT THAN I AM.
DOES HE HAVE A HUMBLE BONE IN HIS BODY?
HE COULD AT LEAST GIVE ME SOME OF HIS PAY TO ME AS AN ALLOWANCE...
HM ?
Sniff sniff
PERFUME ?
MUSK ?
PSHHHHHH
KLAK
PSHHHH
PSHHHHH
IS THIS THE GUY WHO'S WEARING MUSK?
PSHHHHHH
He's washing his hair here?
WHO IS THIS GUY? LONG BROWN HAIR...
Never seen him before
YO, I WANT TO WASH MY HANDS. THINK YOU COULD MO—
Hm?
HEY

ON MY HEAD!
UH, OKAY...

WHY DO I HAVE TO DO THIS FOR HIM?
SCRUB
SCRUB
Ah, that's good.

WHO IS HE, ANYWAY?


DAMMIT, HE'S STARTING TO GET ON MY NERVES...

HEY, YOU.

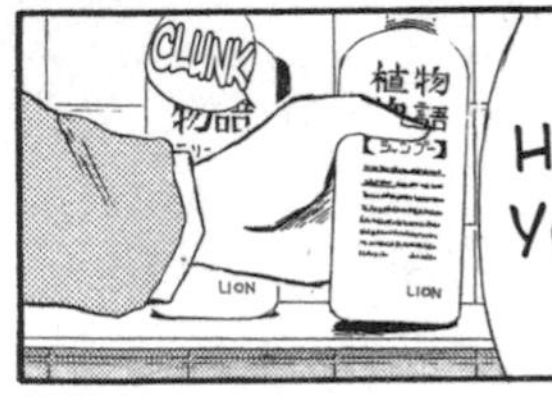


DON'T GET COCKY JUST 'CAUSE I'M NOT TALKING BACK.

I WANNA WASH MY HANDS, SO HURRY UP AND MOVE OUT OF THE WAY!

SCRUB SCRUB

THE CONDITIONER.

WRONG ANSWER, PUNK!
WHAP
SPLISH
!
HEY, WAIT! YOU!
BAM
HUH?
SKRR RRR
HEY, PUNK! ARE YOU GONNA RUN AWAY?!
DON'T JUST RUN AWAY IF YOU'RE A MAN!
Ass-hole!
BPWAA WAM
DAMN, THAT PUNK PISSES ME OFF.
YO! WHAT'S UP, EIKICHI?
You feel like shooting hoops yet?
HAVE YOU SEEN ANY GUY AT THIS SCHOOL WITH LONG BROWN HAIR?
HUH?

DUNNO. IF YOU GO DOWN TO SHIBUYA OR SOMEWHERE YOU'LL FIND PLENTY, THOUGH.
UH HUH.

AN R1-Z ??
THAT MUSK-WEARING PUNK ??

KEH! WHO CARES, ANYWAY.

NEXT TIME I SEE HIM, IT'S THE TURD ATTACK.
Feh heh heh heh
He'll find out what happens when he makes me mad!
what the hell is that?

Let me go find some turds.
You're stepping in one right now.
Gaack!

CLINK CLINK

WELCOME!
!

Y-YOU ?

IT'S BEEN A WHILE, MACHIRUDA BOY.
AND WHAT BRINGS YOU HERE?
I'M HERE TO CLAIM IT.
SOMETHING OF MY OLDER BROTHER'S.
!
ARE YOU STILL
CHASING AFTER HER?
THAT WOMAN
EILEEN?
!
THAT DOESN'T CONCERN YOU.
ALL YOU NEED TO DO IS SHUT UP AND HAND IT OVER.

GOD, WHAT'S WITH THAT GUY?
WHO CARES. MUST BE A SENIOR OR SOME-THING
Forget him.
...
ANYWAY, LET'S HURRY UP AND ROAST THESE SWEET POTA-TOES!
...
These look good! Nothing like sweet potatoes in the winter.
I'M FEELING STARVED!
LISTEN, HE TOLD ME TO POUR SHAMPOO ON HIS HEAD. ME!!
Shampoo
What's wrong with helping him out?
It's about pride!
You have any?
HM?

HEH
I FOUND THAT BAS-TARD'S RI-Z!
HEH HEH
I'M GONNA PLANT THESE TURDS.
HEH HEH
He'll have to give up his bike!
This is revenge! I get scary when you mess with me, see?! Heheh...
HAA-HAHA! NOW HE'LL NEVER BE ABLE TO GET ON HIS BIKE!
Some-times I just don't get this guy...
...

PHEW, I FEEL WAY BETTER NOW!
Hahahaha!
...
COME ON, LET'S ROAST THOSE SWEET POTA-TOES!
HM?
HEY, EIKICHI, OVER THERE.
HUH?
!

THAT'S HIM...

YOU GOT
A SMOKE?

CLUNK
YO...

HM?
SURE

...
CRACKLE
CRACKLE

SO YOU SURF.
IN THIS COLD WEATHER, TOO. OH, WOW.
ZAW
ZAWW

SAY, YOU'VE GOT SOME NERVE MAKING A FOOL OUT OF ME THIS AFTER-NOON.
HEY!

YOU LISTEN-ING TO ME?!
GRAB

ZIP
?!
L-LOOK AT THIS GUY'S BODY!
SCARS? HOW MANY IS THAT?
WHO IS THIS GUY?

...
...
HE —

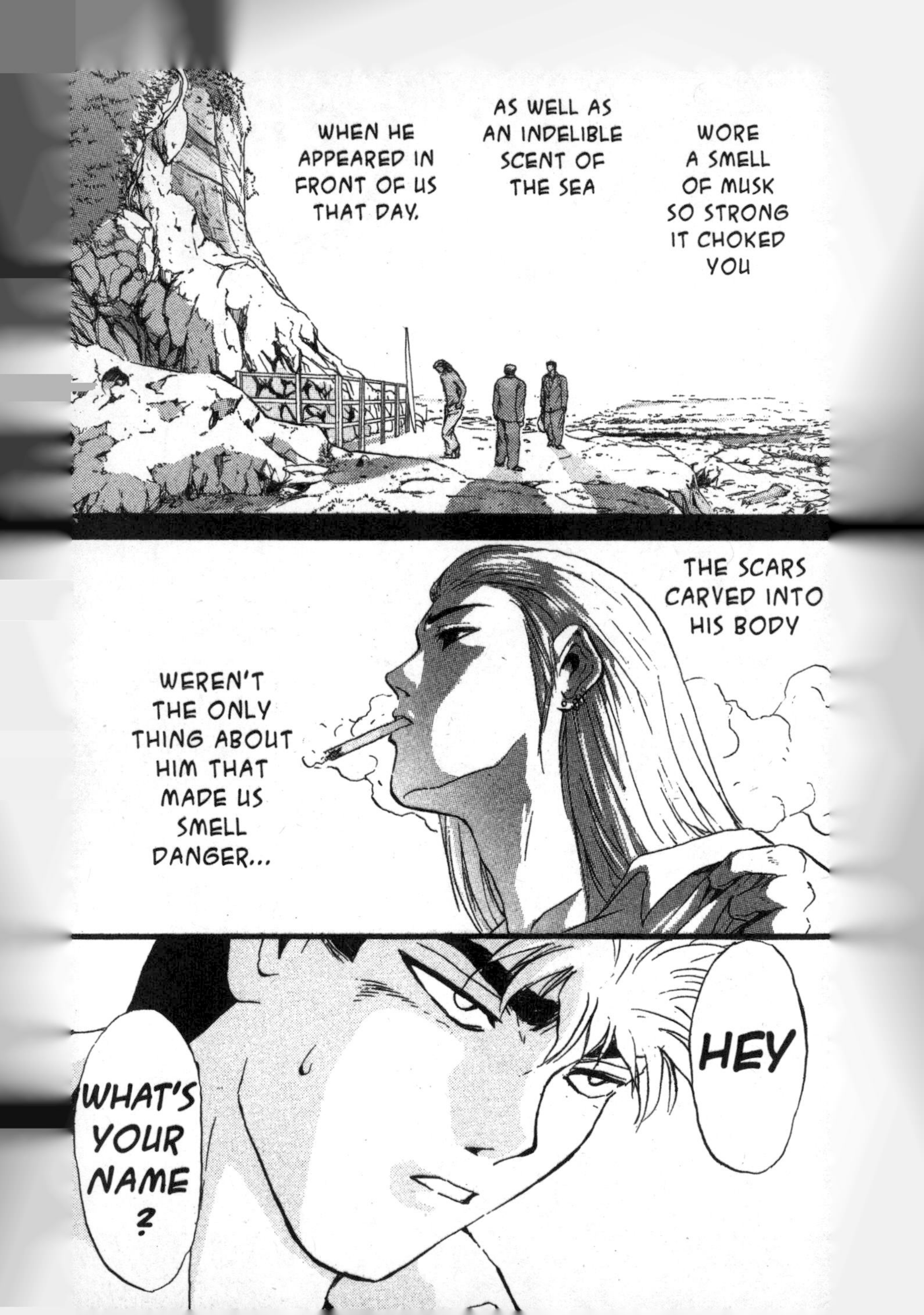
WORE A SMELL OF MUSK SO STRONG IT CHOKED YOU
AS WELL AS AN INDELIBLE SCENT OF THE SEA
WHEN HE APPEARED IN FRONT OF US THAT DAY.
THE SCARS CARVED INTO HIS BODY
WEREN'T THE ONLY THING ABOUT HIM THAT MADE US SMELL DANGER...
HEY
WHAT'S YOUR NAME ?

MA-FUYU...
A STORM WAS CERTAINLY COMING
TO THIS DEEP-WINTER SEA.
MA-FUYU AOKI.

FWMMMM
HEY, EIKICHI! WHAT DO YOU THINK ABOUT THAT GUY FROM YESTER-DAY?
HUH?
YOU KNOW, THAT "MAFUYU" GUY OR WHAT-EVER!

OH, THE SURFER? WHAT ABOUT HIM?!
YOU SAW HIM, DIDN'T YOU?! THOSE SCARS? AND HIS BUILD?

HE'S NOT JUST ANY RANDOM GUY!
HE'S GOT TO BE DANGER-OUS!!

I'VE GOT A BAD FEELING ABOUT HIM...

FMM MM
PWM MM

HE SEEMS LIKE HE MIGHT DO SOMETHING CRAZY!

HEH. SO WHAT IF TURD-BOY DOES?

RYUJI! LET'S BATTLE FROM HERE TO THE SCHOOL!
Wha-at?
LOSER PAYS FOR LUNCH, OKAY?!

I DON'T CARE WHAT SORT OF GUY HE IS.

SKRR
SKRR
I'll take him on !!
BRT
GTO The Early Years
Chapter 215:
TODAY'S NEIGHBOR

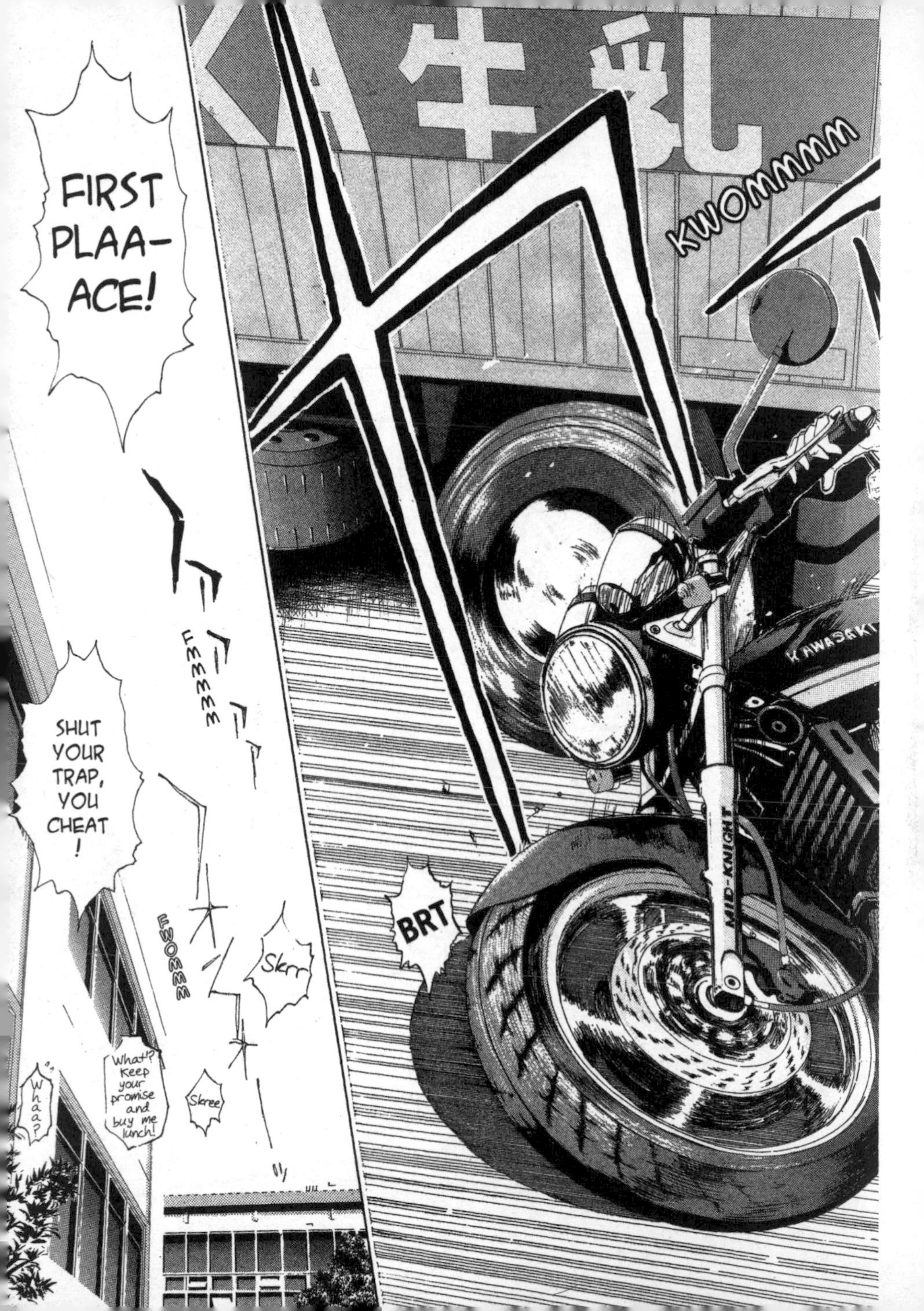
KWOMMMM
KAWASAKI
MID-KNIGHT
BRT
FIRST PLAA-ACE!
FMMMMM
SHUT YOUR TRAP, YOU CHEAT!
FWOMMM
Skrr
Skree
What!? Keep your promise and buy me lunch!
Whaa?

GOD, CBX'S ARE SLOW!
Gotta brush up on your skills.
DUMBASS, YOU BUTTED INTO MY PATH.
HM?
Wanna go?
MUMBLE
CHATTER

HEY, WHAT'S UP?
OH, EI-KICHI!
!
SOME WEIRD GUY IS SITTING IN YOUR SEAT...
WHAT?

MUT-TER
WHIS-PER

THAT'S... THE SURFER FROM YESTER-DAY...
...
FWIP

WHAT'RE YOU DOING HERE?
HAH? C'MON, SURFER BOY!

WANT TO STEP IN SOME TURDS AGAIN?
...
THIS IS MY SEAT, SO GET OUT OF THE DAMN WAY!

GRAB

POM


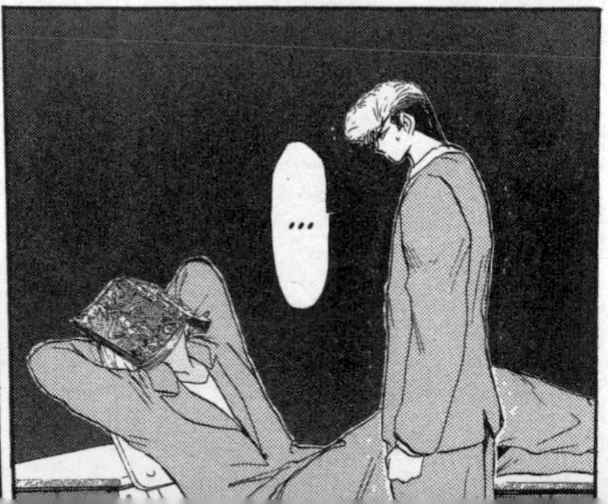

...

HEY, YOU MESSING WITH ME, YOU LITTLE PRICK?
DO YOU HAVE ANY IDEA WHO I AM? HEY!!

You listening to me ?!
Huuuh?
GRAB
CAN YOU SHUT UP?
I'M TRYING TO SLEEP SO BE QUIET, YOU DUMB APE.

APE ??
Twitch twitch

SWIPE
THUD

THWUMP
BLOPBT

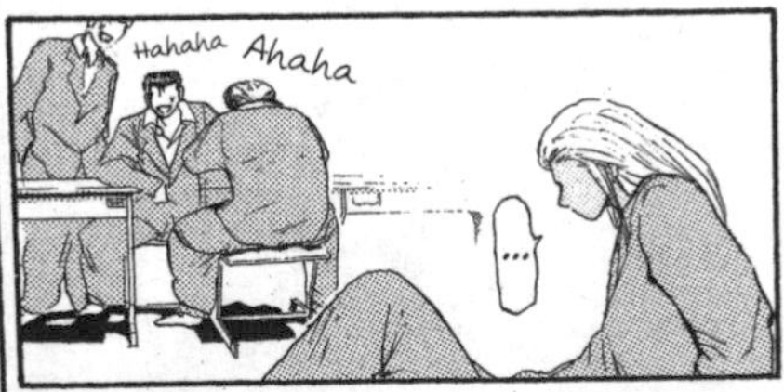
Hahaha Ahaha
...

...
♪

You damn long-haired bas-tard!!
JERK

SLIP
BANG
POP

GRIP
BAM

KREE

TWITCH
Stop it right now!

WHAT ARE YOU DOING, EIKICHI? HONESTLY, IT'S NOT EVEN NOON!
Oh, it's Ms. Mariko!
DO YOU WANT TO GET HELD BACK FOR ANOTHER YEAR, HMM?

DO SOMETHING, MARIKO! THIS LONG-HAIRED APE FROM GOD KNOWS WHERE SHOWS UP AND—
WHO ARE YOU CALLING MARIKO? IT'S MS. IZUMO TO YOU!
POW

YOU MUST BE MAFU-YU?
I'M MARIKO IZUMO, AND I'M CURRENTLY IN CHARGE OF THIS CLASS.

SO YOU FINALLY FELT LIKE COMING TO SCHOOL...
I WEL-COME YOU, TOO.
YO, MARIKO! WHAT ARE YOU GOING ON ABOUT? HURRY UP AND GET THIS STRANGER OUT OF HERE!
HE'S IN YOUR CLASS, DOLT!

WHAT?
TH-THIS GUY
IS IN OUR CLASS?
Hmph
YOU BE NICE TO HIM, EIKICHI. OKAY?
Heh heh

RIGHT, HE'LL BE SITTING NEXT TO YOU FROM TODAY.
YOU SERIOUS, MARIKO? THERE'S NO FREAKING WAY!
This long-haired surfer dude...

SHARE YOUR TEXT-BOOK WITH HIM, EIKICHI.
?!

WHAT, WON'T YOU DO AS I SAY,
ohohoho

EIKICHI "NOT NEARLY ENOUGH ATTENDANCE" ONIZUKA?

COME ON, SHAKE HANDS.
...

HEY!!
SMACK
...
...
Thumbtacks

DOOOOM
Pfff-ft

TO THINK YOU WERE IN MY CLASS ...
...
SO YOU WEREN'T COMING TO SCHOOL? I GUESS IT EXPLAINS MY NOT KNOWING WHO YOU WERE.

YOU LISTENING? MY NAME'S ONIZUKA, AND I RUN THIS PLACE.
MESS WITH ME, AND YOU'LL BE MAKING AN ENEMY OUT OF THE WHOLE SCHOOL.

YOU BETTER NOT PUSH ME, FOR YOUR OWN SAKE.
GOT IT, WINTER-BOY?

SILENCE
...

H-HE'S NOT LISTEN-ING!!
This just makes me look like the loser here!!
Like some twit!

H-HEY, I'M GIVING YOU ADVICE SO THAT YOU DON'T GET BULLIED ...
HM ?
Scribble

SCRIBBLE
WHAT ARE YOU DOING SCRIBBLING IN MY TEXT-BOOK?!

SNATCH
GIVE IT BACK!

GRAB

Y-YOU BAS-TARD!
RRIP
KREE

WHAM

Haaaah?!
WHAT'S SO FUNNY, PUNK? HUH??
I'll kill you, bas-tard!
Hey, Eiki-chi!
THUD
Pffffff
BAM
STOP IT RIGHT NOW!!
Pff
...
TOILET

HEY. YOU BETTER GET WISE.

DON'T GET TOO BIG OF A HEAD, NOW.
EIKICHI'S PRETTY KIND, SO HE MIGHT NOT BEAT YOU UP ...
I'll stand watch!

BUT WE'RE NOT QUITE AS MATURE.
THERE'S NO TELLING WHAT WE MIGHT DO. UNDER-STAND?
LISTEN UP. YOU BETTER SHOW UP TOMORROW WITH A SHAVED HEAD
THEN GET ON ALL FOURS AND APOLOGIZE TO EIKICHI. GOT IT?

HEY, YOU LISTEN-ING TO ME?!
GRAB
FACE ME WHEN I'M TALKING TO YOU!

BSHHH

GAAAAAAAH?!
SPLISH

Why the hell did you face me?!!
SWING

BOOM
GRAB

K...
SWING
KATSU ?!

HALT!!
ズ
SLIDE
A- ARE YOU OKAY?
HEY, KATSU-YUKI!!
SLUMP

I'M NOT PULLING THE NEXT PUNCH.
GOT IT?
Y-YOU BASTARD... WHAT ARE YOU PULLING PUNCHES FOR?
DON'T TAKE US LIGHTLY!
WE CAN FIGHT ONE ON ONE, JUST CHOOSE SOME-ONE.
WHAT DO YOU SAY? HUH?
Bas-tard...
FSHHH

SQUEEK
WIPE

BASTAAAARD!!

WAAAGH?! KATSU!!

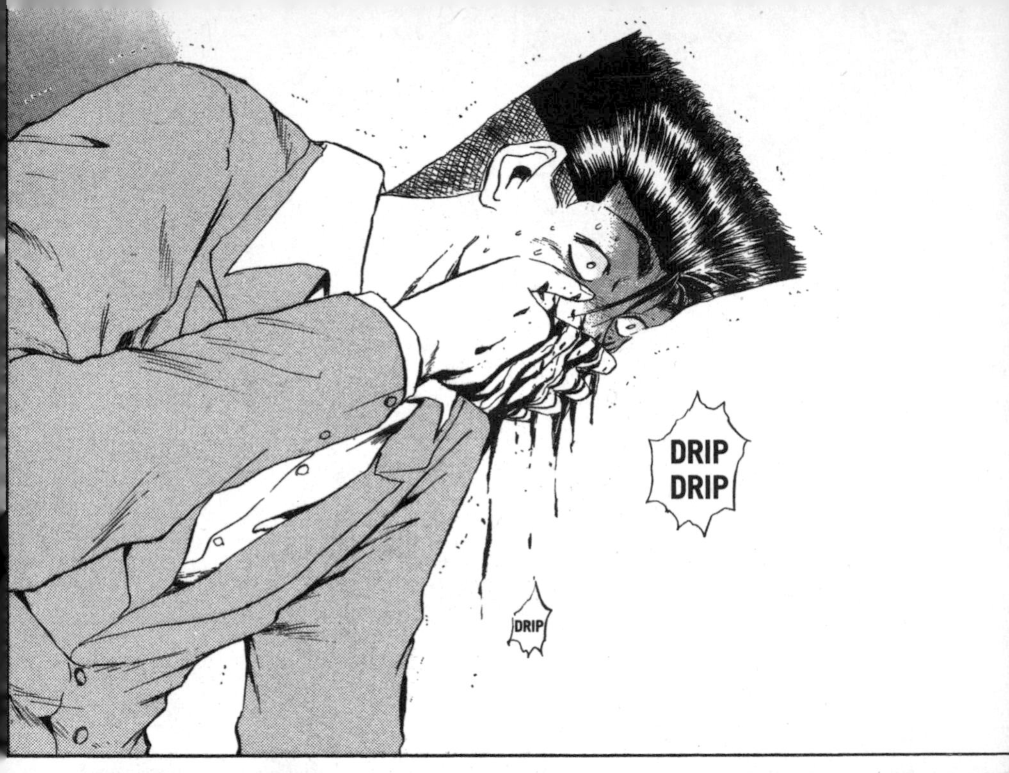
DRIP
DRIP
DRIP

WHA ...?
A NOSE-BLEED?

DIDN'T HE HALT THAT PUNCH?
WHY IS HE BLEED-ING?
COULD THE SHEER FORCE OF THE PUNCH HAVE ...?!

WH ...
WHO IS THAT GUY?

HEY! WHAT ARE YOU KIDS DOING? CLASS HAS ALREADY STAR...
Ack!
WAIT, WHAT HAPPENED THERE? WHY'S HIS NOSE BLEEDING?

IT'S NOTHING. I JUST FELT SOME BLOOD RUSH TO MY HEAD ...
I'LL HEAD RIGHT BACK TO CLASS.

HEY, AFTERNOON TODAY IS P.E., ISN'T IT?
Tch! Hurry up!
YEAH ... WHY?

We're doing judo now, right?
Per-fect.

LISTEN, YOU BETTER NOT TELL EIKICHI ABOUT THIS.
LET EVERYONE IN THE P.E. CLASS KNOW

US FRESHMEN... WILL TAKE CARE OF HIM.

Hmph
We'll set him right with some *real* physical education !!

GTO The Early Years 12: End

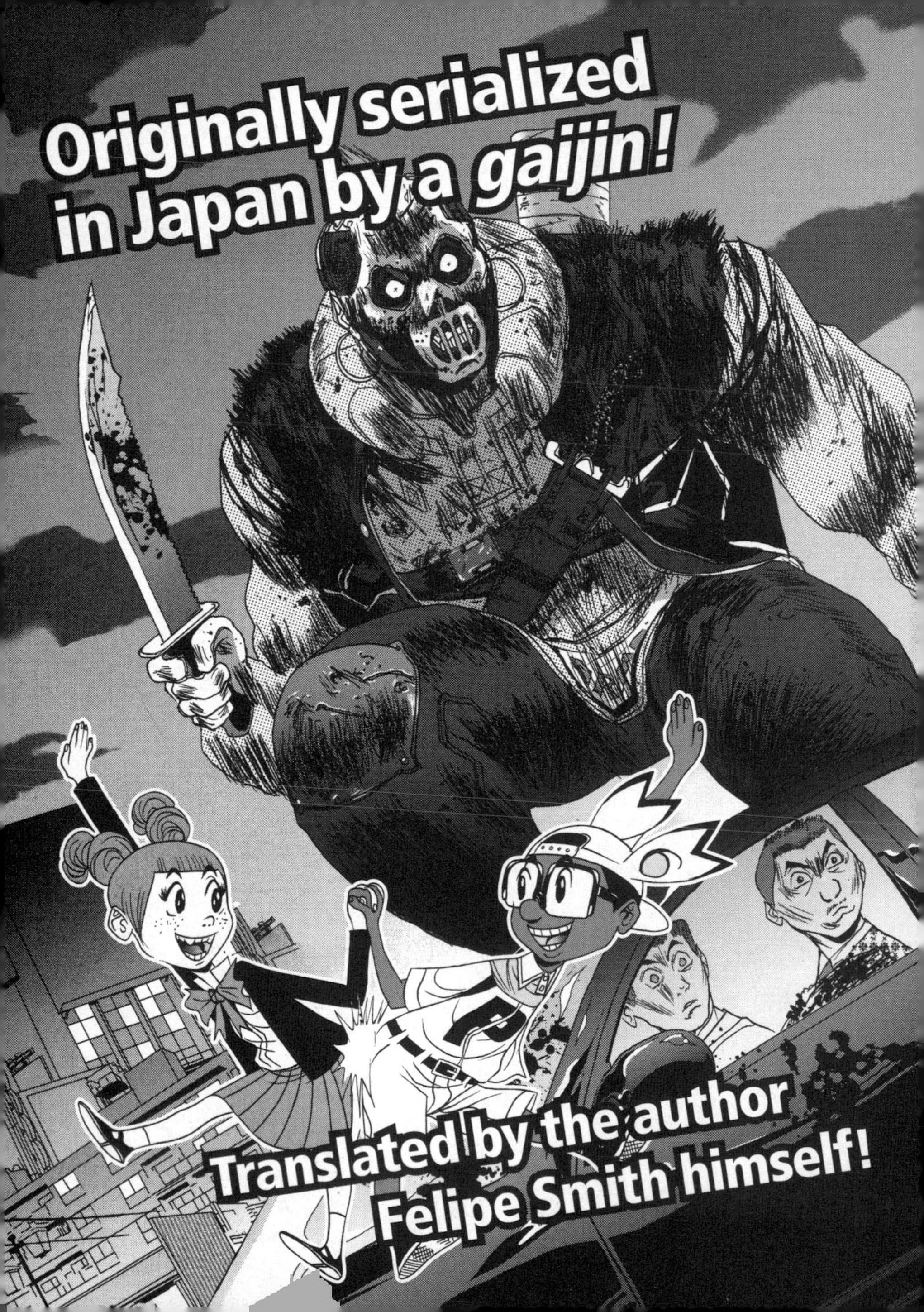
Originally serialized
in Japan by a *gaijin*!
Translated by the author
Felipe Smith himself!

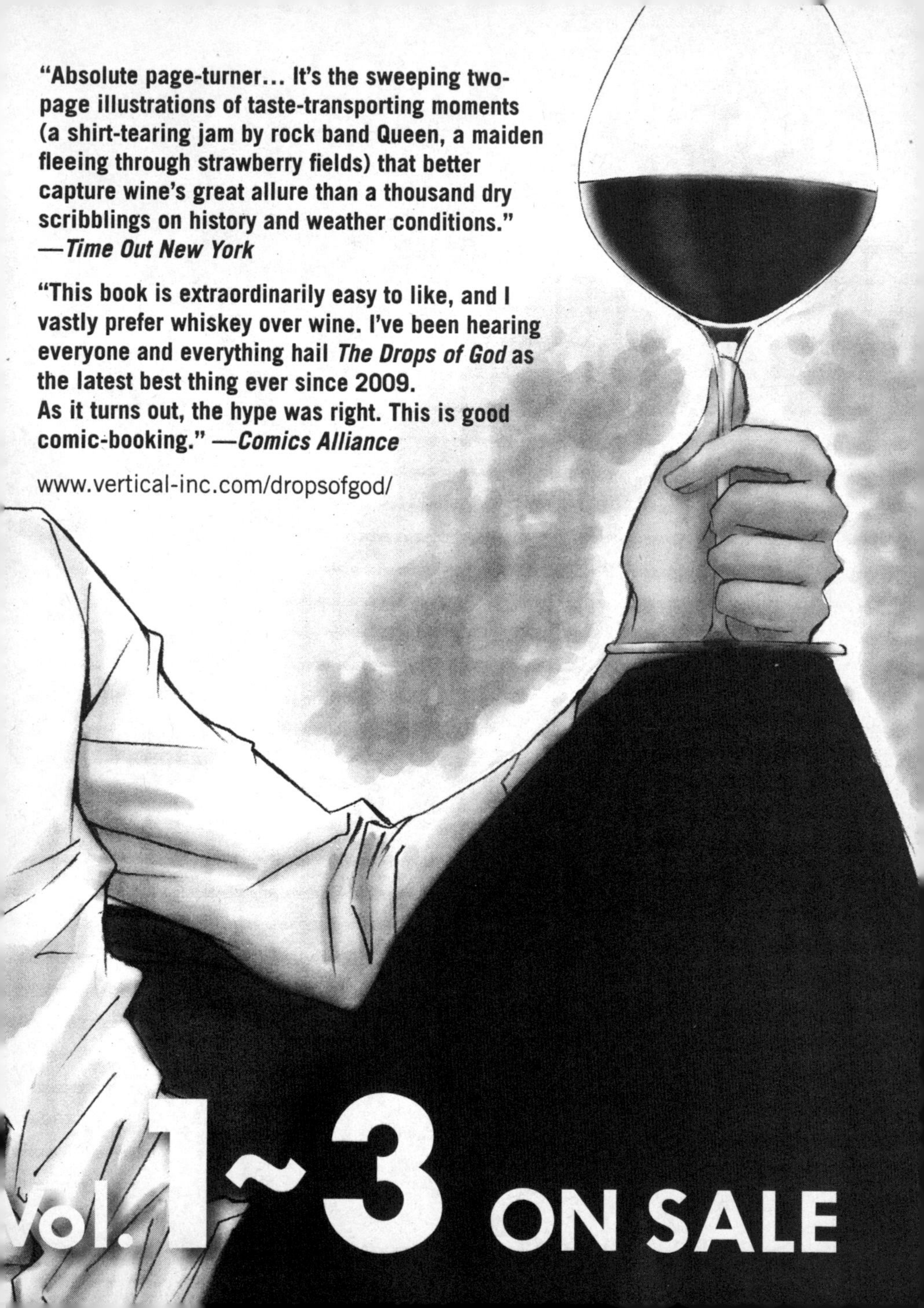

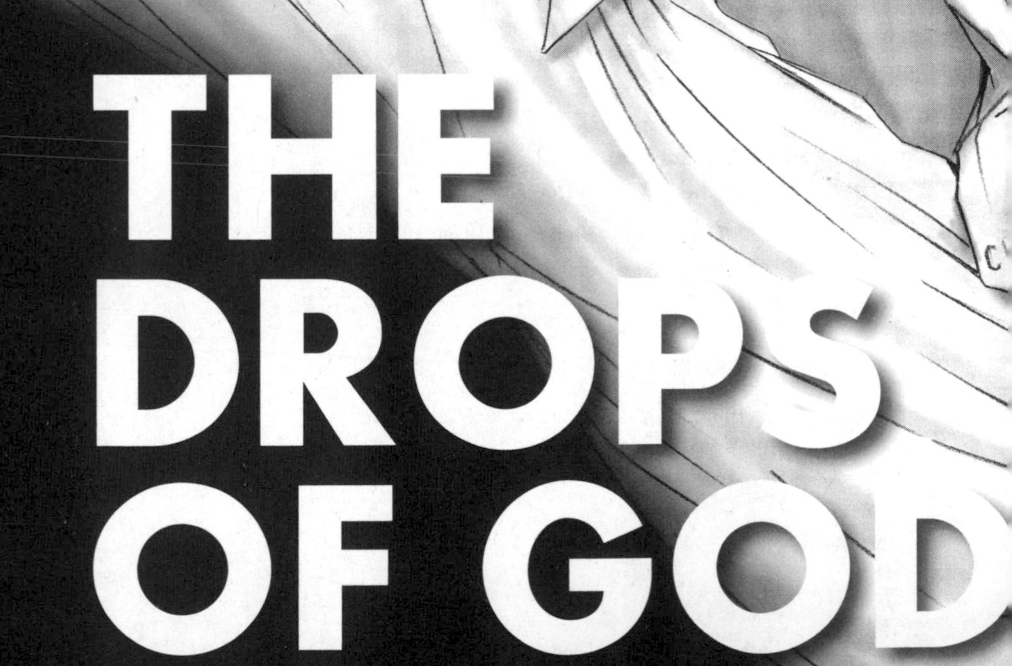
THE
DROPS
OF GOD

**GTO: The Early Years, Volume 12**

Translation: Ko Ransom
Production: Hiroko Mizuno
Nicole Dochych
Tomoe Tsutsumi


First published in Japan in 1995 by Kodansha, Ltd., Tokyo
Publication for this English edition arranged through Kodansha, Ltd., Tokyo
This version is based off the 2005 mass market edition by Kodansha, Ltd.
English language version produced by Vertical, Inc.

Translation provided by Vertical, Inc., 2012
Published by Vertical, Inc., New York

*Shonan Junai-gumi* first serialized in *Shuukan Shonen Magazine*,
Kodansha, Ltd., 1990-1996

This is a work of fiction.

ISBN: 978-1-932234-86-2

Manufactured in the United States of America

First Edition

Vertical, Inc.
451 Park Avenue South
7th Floor
New York, NY 10016
www.vertical-inc.com